Also by Ron Schwab

Sioux Sunrise
Paint the Hills Red
Grit

The Lockes
Last Will
Medicine Wheel
Hell's Fire

The Law Wranglers
Deal with the Devil
Mouth of Hell
The Last Hunt
Summer's Child
Peyote Spirits

The Coyote Saga
Night of the Coyote
Return of the Coyote
Twilight of the Coyote

Hell's Fire

Chapter 1

G RANNY GRAY OWL was starting to get a little spooked by the racket outside her small Kaw-style lodge in the Kansas Flint Hills. This was the third straight night now that she had heard something or someone snooping around outside. She retrieved her double-barreled shotgun from the crude all-purpose table where it always rested, loaded and ready for her to squeeze the trigger. She sat back down in her rocking chair, facing the deerskin-flap that covered the entry opening.

Granny's lodge was a bowl-shaped structure, its slanted walls and beamed, arched roof sheathed with bark slabs and skins. It was built over a circular two-foot-deep excavation so the occupant was required to step up or down upon exiting or entering. There were no windows, and her feeble light sometimes came from a stone fire ring in the center of the room from whence smoke escaped through a hole in the ceiling above. There was no need of a fire for warmth tonight, though, since it was early August and plenty hot enough without adding more heat to it. Thus, she had surrendered to the modern convenience of a flickering kerosene lamp that sat on the table. A few shards of a full moon's glow crept through the smoke-hole and several rips in the lodge's covering.

Earlier she had heard the rustling of brush from the direction of the canyon, but that could have been any of a dozen creatures. This time she thought she picked up the cry of a child. A bobcat or even a cougar, perhaps, although the latter was seldom seen these days.

Granny was several years beyond her ninetieth birthday, a tiny and wizened woman, but not as frail as she appeared. Beneath the buckskin britches and flannel shirt was a wiry, tough woman who still tended to her daily chores and did what she needed to survive in the rugged hill country. She lived a spartan existence in the one-room lodge perched within twenty-five feet from branches of a shallow canyon that bordered the north and west of the structure. The Flint Hills canyons were dwarfs compared to those of the Rockies rising west of the plains, but they still presented travel challenges to man and beast. Here, the sloping canyon walls dropped steeply from the rims on each side to form blunted vees when they met at the rocky floors, where mostly dry streambeds snaked to be awakened only after torrential rains that could not be swallowed by the cracks and crevices in the limestone hills.

The canyons' inclines were covered by gnarled oaks and gooseberry bushes and other vegetation Granny harvested for survival. She enjoyed the luxury of a good well within fifty feet from the lodge to provide her personal water supply. It also furnished a water source for her mule and the dozen goats that grazed on the tallgrass prairie that filled out the portion of her forty acres that was not stolen by the canyons. As the crow flies, the lodge was located slightly more than a mile from the thriving village of Medicine Wheel. But the journey by mule and wagon over the ruts that passed for roads made it nearly a three-mile trip over rolling hills and prairie.

Granny ordinarily thrived on her isolation. She often dropped off to sleep listening to the owls hooting from the darkness of the canyons, the locusts buzzing from the trees or the raccoons scavenging outside the lodge on the chance she might have dropped a morsel some place. Coyote howls usually joined in. She knew these sounds intimately, having listened to them for most of her long lifetime. But the movement and sounds that reached her ears this night did not match those of her usual friends. Something in the night's chorus was off-tune.

Jasper, her old gelded mule, shrieked, and the goats bleated from the log lean-to and pens where she collected them for the night. The critter unrest was not unusual when a coyote or bobcat came prowling. She did not worry about such visitors. Jasper would stomp the life out of any small creature that might dig under the log, stockade-type fence with hewn points rimming the top. A cougar would cause a bigger ruckus. She wondered for a moment if the mewling she had heard might have come from the goat pen. The kids' bleating sometimes sounded like the crying of a child, and her hearing was not so keen anymore, fading even more quickly than her eyesight.

Then, the cries erupted again, and this time the pitiful noise came from just outside the entrance, sending shivers down her spine. She tightened her fingers on the shotgun's stock, resting her right elbow on the rocking chair's arm and propping up the heavy barrels with her left hand to level the weapon at the entry opening.

"Hello, Miss Gray Owl. Visitors," came a muffled, raspy voice.

"Who are you?"

"Doesn't matter. Me and my little girl just came by to introduce ourselves."

"Strange time to visit. Let me see the little girl."

"I'll send her in. Gina, honey, you just go in and show yourself to the nice lady."

Granny could hear a girl sobbing, "No, I won't. You're not my daddy, and you want to hurt her."

The slap of hand against flesh. "Get the hell in there, you little pissant."

A wild-eyed, dirty-faced little girl in a tattered dress stumbled through the opening and fell the several feet to the recessed floor. This distracted Granny for a moment.

"Put your gun down," came the man's voice from outside.

"Go to hell," croaked Granny. She squeezed the trigger, and the shotgun roared like thunder off the walls of the closed-in room.

The recoil almost knocked her out of the rocker, and, before she could recover her balance and fire again, a slim black-hooded figure leapt through the opening, wrested the shotgun from her hands and tipped over the rocker, dumping her onto the dirt floor. "That's enough, you stinking old squaw. Tell me where you keep the money, and I'll be on my way."

"Got no money."

That earned her a sharp kick in the ribs, and the pain shot through her body the instant she felt the give of bone. "Don't lie. You been selling your medicines and potions for years for gold and silver coins. Don't spend nothing but a penny now and then. Folks say you got a good amount of money stashed. I aim to find out where if it takes all night. I know how to make you hurt in ways you never dreamed of."

"Help me up, and I will show you where I hide the money."

The intruder bent over and grabbed a bony hand and elbow and hoisted the ancient woman to her feet. With an agility that belied the feeble look of her body, Granny's nimble fingers closed about the homemade handle of the ice pick she had secreted in her trouser belt, and she drove the point into the tender flesh between the attacker's neck and shoulder. The would-be thief screamed and reflexively released her, dropping her on the floor again, then drew a holstered Colt and fired a shot into Granny Gray Owl's head.

Chapter 2

Doctor Thaddeus Locke was nearly finished stitching up the ear and jaw of a Redbone Coonhound that had lost a fight earlier in the evening to a cornered boar raccoon. The owner, Charlie King, steadied the male hound on the surgery table, but the tough, stoic animal did not even flinch as the Medicine Wheel veterinarian inserted the surgical needle into his flesh and pulled the catgut suture through to close the wounds. The hapless dog seemed more embarrassed than anything else as the thickset, black-bearded hunter chided him for letting the coon get the best of him.

"All done, Charlie," Thad said, as he began cleaning his surgical tray. "We don't do anything with the stitches. They'll disintegrate on their own. But let me know if there is any pus or sign of infection. And don't hunt him until he's healed up."

"I won't. Got me one of them Bluetick hounds from Louisiana. I'll give her a try. Maybe she can teach old Red here a thing or two. Plan to breed them and see what they come up with."

"Well, his injuries shouldn't keep him from doing his part in that process whenever she comes in heat."

Charlie lifted the Redbone off the table and headed for the door, the dejected dog following at his heels. "Dun me for this, will you, Doc?"

"Okay, Charlie." Thad knew he wouldn't see payment for six months or better, but Charlie was good for it. Approaching fifty, Charlie had a small farm along the river bottom that produced well when Charlie got around to planting and harvesting. He earned a subsistence living from a potentially productive farm because his coon dogs and fishing tended to come first. This could be troublesome when a man had a wife and eight kids to support. Fortunately, his sixteen-year-old son, Andy, was a bright youngster and a hard worker and seemed to be on his way to taking over the farming. Perhaps, Charlie had sired a better future.

No sooner had Charlie left the Locke Vet Hospital than a frantic barking outside the front door broke out. He instantly recognized the bark as Cinder's and moved quickly to the door and opened it. The sinewy Dalmatian

bitch saw him and turned toward the northeast and continued barking. Thad looked that direction and immediately saw what the commotion was about. A firestorm
appeared to have erupted against the backdrop of a char-
coal-hued sky, more sparks than flames shooting into
the heavens. The source came from one of the hills above
Medicine Wheel, which was set in the Big Blue River Val-
ley. He ran a quick inventory in his mind of the outlying
farms and ranches. There were not many. This had to be
Granny Gray Owl's.

Thad raced across the dusty street to the town's new
fire hall where a single pump wagon and new Studebaker
freight wagon were stored adjacent to an attached stable
housing a pair of thick-chested, muscular bay geldings to
pull the pump wagon and a team of mules for the freight
wagon. The Studebaker was stocked with buckets, axes,
shovels, ladders and other fire-fighting equipment. The
pump wagon, in addition to the hand pump, carried a
small tank of water and hose that could either be utilized
with the pump to suck water from the tank or dropped
into a nearby well or creek to suck the precious liquid
from the sources.

Thad grabbed the rope suspended from the old school
bell bolted to the long pole in front of the limestone building and began pulling. The bell shut out all other sound

for several minutes until he released the rope. He called for Cinder, who had disappeared to calm the fire hall's equine occupants while the bell tolled. The mysterious ability to quiet and relax horses, seemingly unique to the Dalmatian breed, was why the dogs were used by fire departments on the East Coast. Cinder had been purchased by Thad as a pup from a St. Louis breeder. Training her to follow her own instincts had been surprisingly easy.

Cinder raced toward him as he turned to open the fire hall doors so he could lead the mule and horse teams from the stable to start hitching them to the wagons. He anticipated other brigade volunteers would be joining him within minutes. He paused and took Cinder's head and gently pointed her nose in the direction of the fire. "Cinder," he said. "Fire. Go."

The dog rocketed down the road heading for the fire and disappeared into the trees and undergrowth that fringed the east side of the little town. Normally Cinder would race ahead of the horses or ride in the wagon, but Thad knew they were making this run to prevent the fire from spreading to either the canyon timber or the tallgrass prairie beyond. If the sparks and flames were shooting from Granny Gray Owl's lodge, as he suspected, it would be long gone by the time the volunteers arrived. Cinder, on the other hand, had rescue capabilities if needed.

It was no surprise that Kirsten Cavelle was the first arrival at the station. Medicine Wheel was a company town owned by Medicine Wheel Properties Incorporated of which Kirsten was the major, but not yet controlling, shareholder. As company president she had made it clear the funds would not be available for construction of the station and purchase of the equipment if her application for membership in the volunteer fire brigade should be declined. There had been grumbling among some of the older members, but what was a fire brigade with nothing but a few buckets?

Kirsten nodded at him and headed directly for the stable to retrieve the horses and mules. He followed the tall, slender woman with endless denim-covered legs that disappeared into well-worn cowboy boots. They had been lovers for months until he proposed marriage six months back. She had replied, "I'd have to think about that."

After that night she had begun to pull back, and their all-night trysts had ended, and their relationship had descended into occasional, brief conjugal visits in one or the other's bed. He kicked aside any further thought of marriage. Did he still love her? He did not doubt that he did, but he had lost at that game another time and was not going to press for more hurt. He could not subdue his desire for her, though, and she never left any doubt she still lusted for him—when she felt the need, and a get-together didn't interfere with business. Their future together was suspended in limbo, which was complicated further by the tangle of business enterprises they partnered in.

Three more volunteers showed up as they were leading the horses and mules to the wagons. Red Holiday, a stocky, muscular man with thick hair and beard that earned his nickname, already had harnesses and tack for the mules in hand and took one of the mules from Thad. They hitched Cain and Abel, the twin gelded mules, to the Studebaker, while Kirsten and the others readied the horses.

Red tacked a note on the bell pole informing latecomers where the brigade was going, and Kirsten, taking the reins of the horse team, pulled out with one volunteer in the seat beside her and a mounted volunteer close behind. Red drove the mule team since he ran a freighting operation and clearly held an edge over the others when it came to handling the mules. Thad joined him on the double seat, and in a few minutes, they caught up with

Kirsten's pump wagon. By this time several more horse-back riders had fallen in with the convoy.

Red was the brigade's elected fire chief and issued the orders when he was available for fire combat. A former cavalry sergeant stationed at nearby Fort Riley when he mustered out, Red started up his own freight business with a single team and wagon and now operated more than twenty wagons fulfilling military contracts for enterprises based in Medicine Wheel and Manhattan, sometimes handling loads to and from Topeka more than fifty miles east of Manhattan. Red was in his early forties, and Thad figured the business was just getting started. He was also Thad's best veterinary client.

As they bounced over the rough trail that snaked into the Flint Hills, Red said, "You said it is Granny's place. I assume Kirsten knows the way?"

"She said she does. It's likely she's tried to buy the place. Outside the canyon, except what little Granny's goats and mule eat, it's almost virgin tallgrass."

"Not sure you can be almost virgin, Doc. Either are or you ain't."

Thad thought about the remark. "Yeah, I guess you got me on that one. Anyway, Kirsten's always looking to buy good grass on the cheap."

"Ain't seen you and Kirsten together so much lately. You still wooing her?"

"I never thought of myself as wooing her. We still socialize a bit. But I don't think she's the marrying kind."

Red laughed. "Socializing. Now that's a new name for it. I'll have to use that one on Molly."

Thad was glad darkness was settling in because he could feel the heat on his face and neck. He changed the subject. "When's Molly due?"

"About two months. Early October. Will you help if the midwife has trouble?"

"Red, I'm a vet. A horse doctor. Do you think Molly wants her fifth child delivered by a vet?"

"You help folks in emergencies. You are a licensed human doctor. Even if you wasn't, I'd trust you with my Molly and the little one. It takes too long to get her to Manhattan, or to get Doc Gordon out here."

"If there seems to be a problem, track me down, and I'll see if I can help."

"Thanks, Doc. I feel better knowing that."

Most of the Lockes were congenital lawyers. His father, Myles Franklin Locke, sometimes referred to as "the Judge" in deference to his service as an Illinois appellate judge before the death of his first wife, had moved with three young sons to Kansas with other Free Staters during the mid-1850s. Thad and twin sister, Hannah, were Kansas-born to Myles Locke's second wife, Deborah Compton Locke, who died giving birth on July 4, 1855. The new babies had been surrendered to their childless mother's sister, Nancy Clay, and her husband, Eldridge, and raised on the Clay Flint Hills ranch, seeing their lawyer father mostly Sundays until high school, when they stayed with him weekdays in Manhattan.

The eldest of the children, identical twins Ian and Cam, had both taken up law wrangling, as had sister Hannah, who partnered in a law firm in Wyoming and only rarely visited. Cam practiced law in Manhattan with their father, and Ian was a lawyer-banker in Nebraska. Middle child Franklin was a Methodist circuit preacher in western Nebraska. Thad's heart lay with creatures great and small in his beloved Kansas Flint Hills, and he supposed his ranch upbringing had contributed to that. He had aspired to be a veterinarian as far back as he could recall, and he nursed injured and sick animals through his high school years. There were no veterinary schools when he turned nineteen, and he could have simply self-declared his occupation, but, at the Judge's urging, he had enrolled at the University of Pennsylvania medical school for the several years required to procure a medical degree.

While he was duly licensed to practice medicine in the state of Kansas, he considered himself first and foremost a veterinarian. Iowa State Agricultural College now offered a veterinary degree program, but when the 1887 fall term at Manhattan's Kansas State Agricultural College started in another month there would be a decent offering of animal health courses, and he was confident a full veterinary curriculum would be established within a decade. He would have leaped at the animal-specialized education if one had been available. Fortunately, the knowledge required to care for animals and humans was generally transferable from one patient to the other.

Red broke the long silence that had passed between them. "Doc, Kirsten's leaving the trail and heading into the tallgrass. I guess I'll just assume she knows where she's headed."

"Do you want to challenge her?"

"Not me."

" It's likely a shortcut she knows about. I've been out to Granny's many times but never gone this way. The broken trail's rough, but at least we can see what's under the horses and wagons. I just worry about a hidden gopher hole or wash in the tallgrass."

The wagon bounced and came down hard. "Damn rocks don't make the ride any smoother," Red grumbled.

They were rolling at a faster pace, though, and Thad could see the flames engulfing the lodge not more than fifteen minutes away. Kirsten was shaving a half hour off the journey with her recklessness. He had heard some, out of the feisty woman's hearing, call her "Crazy Kirsten." She could be crazy. He knew that from his own experience with her. But mostly like a fox.

Chapter 3

C INDER STOOD AT the edge of the smoldering lodge when the wagons and riders arrived, barking frantically at something in the glowing coals in what looked like a giant barbecue pit. Most of the lodge's covering had disintegrated and dropped to the floor or disappeared as ash flakes in the late summer breeze. Sparks were no longer spitting into the sky, and fortunately the fire had been contained to the clearing around the buildings and had not yet spread to the prairie grass or the canyon that twisted behind the lodge.

Red hollered orders to the fire warriors, "Kirsten, get your crew to work with the pump and hose on the lodge and then wet down the ground around the place. When you use up the water in the tank, see if you can get a hose down the well and pump the water from there.

Everybody else, help try to clear the rubble. Cinder thinks Granny's in the lodge."

Thad thought that if Granny was in the lodge there was no hope for her. The dugout below the structure had collected all the fiery residue. They all retrieved their heavy canvas coats and the thick, leather helmets from the wagon box, and after donning the gear, they moved quickly to the tasks they had practiced many times during weekly drills.

Kirsten ordered two men to the pump and two others to stretch the hose to the smoking remnants of the structure while she maneuvered the other end of the hose into the tarp-covered livestock tank that sat on the rear of the pump wagon. When the hose started sucking up the water, she jumped off the wagon and raced to the well with a small axe and began to tear away enough of the frame cover to allow admittance to the water when the tank was empty. The small pump that rested on top of the frame would never yield enough water to douse the fire.

Thad, Red and J. B. Hall, an apprentice meat-smoker at Quincy Belmont's meat processing operation in Medicine Wheel, hurried to the edge of the disintegrating lodge, where Cinder continued to bark. Red yelled, "Kirsten, get the water over here."

"Give us a damn minute," she retorted.

And it seemed a minute was all she needed, for lithe and sinewy Kirsten, taller than any man there except for Thad, appeared beside them and aimed the nozzle and shot the water at the path carved by Red's hand gestures. The flames and red-hot coals hissed and spat smoke as the water struck. J. B. retrieved shovels and a big axe, and as soon as Kirsten had a path soaked down, she and her crew drug the hose away and moved along the structure's edge.

Red took the lead when they stepped down into the smoking cavity, pushing away the charred timbers and rubble as they inched toward the spot that a still-anxious Cinder identified with her pointing nose. Thad smelled the burnt flesh before he caught sight of the crusty, blackened leg protruding from underneath a fallen beam.

"There's Granny," he said. "It's what I feared. If she had gotten out, she would have been out there some place."

"Let's move the beam and get the body out," Red said.

By the time the three men cleared away the debris, moved the charred corpse onto a canvas tarp, and removed it from the former lodge, Kirsten's crew had doused the fire, and the fire volunteers were wetting-down the adjacent ground. J. B. fetched a kerosene lamp to illuminate the remains.

Thad knelt beside what the fire had left of Granny's scorched body, his eyes studying the silent skeletal form carefully. The flesh on her legs and buttocks had been seared to the bone by the flames, but the skin above the waist, though blistered and scorched, appeared largely intact. It seemed the heavy ceiling beam had inexplicably formed a dividing line between lesser and greater damage. But the injury that gripped Thad's attention was the hole bored into her skull just above her partially burnt-off nose.

Red said, "Is that wound what I think it is?"

"It is if you think it looks like a bullet wound. I'm ninety-five percent certain Granny didn't suffer from the burns or asphyxiation if that's any consolation."

"What do we do?"

"Send somebody to Manhattan for Sheriff Mallery. Tell him he'll probably want to bring the coroner with him."

"That'll take two hours to get there at night. Another two hours back."

"I don't think we've got any choice. We shouldn't move the body or tamper with anything else without Sam Mallery's okay. I'll stay till the Sheriff comes. I'll keep Cinder with me and let her sniff around some more."

"I'll stay with you." The voice was not Red's. "You got your Colt?" Thad did not bother to turn around. He could pick Kirsten's voice out of a screaming crowd.

He got up and faced her. "No. You know I don't carry a pistol."

Kirsten pulled back her canvas coat and patted the butt of the holstered pistol that hung from her gun belt. "I've got mine. I'll stay with you."

He wasn't in the mood to argue with her, and he knew it would be a waste of time, so he said nothing. It annoyed him some that she still carried a sidearm. While many women could handle a rifle, and a few secreted a Deringer in their bags, Kirsten had the dubious distinction of being the only woman in Riley County who wore a gun on her hip. Kansas was nearly civilized these days, and, outside of local lawmen, only a sprinkling of the ranchers and cowboys still carried pistols, mostly to use on copperheads or the smaller massasauga rattlesnakes that were starting to overpopulate the Flint Hills.

Red broke the uncomfortable silence. "We need to get the horses and wagons back to the fire hall in case there'd be another fire some place. I've got a small buckboard over at the freight office, and I'll get a team and driver ready to go with the sheriff if he'll swing by. Want me to get your horses from the livery and send them along?"

"I'd appreciate that, Red. And you'll send somebody to Manhattan to get Sam?"

"Consider it done. Don't worry about a thing. You two just stay here and socialize a bit and get some rest if you can."

Thad ignored Red's futile attempt at humor. And he was not about to socialize with Granny's corpse nearby. This tragedy put his mind far away from what Red was suggesting. He was aware that it would be a scandal to some church ladies in Manhattan if they heard about a man and woman being left behind in the darkness without a chaperone, but the folks of Medicine Wheel and surrounding farms and ranches accepted the unorthodox relationship between Thad and Kirsten. Any who felt compelled to attribute sin generally pointed to Kirsten, who had made herself a widow by killing her husband a few years back. It made no difference he had nearly beaten her to death first.

Chapter 4

THE VOLUNTEERS HAD left two kerosene lanterns behind for Thad and Kirsten, but they were only a few nights shy of a full moon. They agreed to save the lamplight for later in case they came across something of significance that required better light or cloud cover interfered with their viewing. As they walked the ground surrounding the destroyed lodge, Kirsten suddenly stopped. It was so quiet, the only sound coming from the rustling of tree leaves and branches in the canyon.

"Thad?" she called. "Something's missing."

Thad strode toward her from the other side of the pit, Cinder at his booted heels. "What do you mean?" he asked.

"Granny had a small goat herd—a dozen or fifteen animals, I'd guess. And a mule. I haven't heard a sound from them. And I'm sure she penned them up at night."

"I treated the mule once when it came up lame. Had a cut that had screwworms working on it. And I've done vet work on the goats a few times. There were goats grazing around the place when I rode out for medicines I few weeks back. She hadn't stopped at the clinic for a spell, and I had run short on several of her salves."

Kirsten rushed to the stockade-fence that enclosed the rickety shed on the edge of the building site. She unlatched the gate and swung it open. Empty. She entered and strolled around the lot, eyes fastened to the ground. When she came out, she picked up a stick and began to scrape her boot sole. "Fresh goat shit," she said. "Granny still had goats. Mule apples, too."

"What's your point? Goat rustlers? Maybe the animals are out in the tallgrass."

"I know you don't doctor many goats, but they're damn curious critters. They should have shown up here by now if they were out in the grass. They'd want to see what was going on. We can check come daylight, but I'm betting they're gone."

"So, you think whoever killed Granny stole the mule and goats?"

"I'm just saying it's a possibility. Or they drove off the critters some place to throw us off their trail. It could mean something or nothing at all."

"She was a strange little lady. I knew her since I was a kid no more than ten years old. I came up here with Uncle El to buy medicines and salves for cattle and horses. She brewed stuff from herbs and roots that were far more effective than most of the commercial products available. Later, when I showed interest in caring for animals, she taught me about some of her remedies, and after I came back and started my practice, I probably became her best customer. Whenever she drove her wagon to town she stopped at the clinic with an inventory of her concoctions for animals and humans, and I always bought a few things."

"Did she have medical training?"

"Not that I'm aware of. I'm told she was a Kaw medicine woman and learned her skills from the tribe's shamans and medicine people. She claimed to have lived in the Blue Earth Village, the home of the Kansa or Kaw Indians some fifty or sixty years ago, before the tribe was removed to a reservation village. The city of Manhattan sits on the village site now. Under treaties with the government, the Kaw were first moved east of Manhattan and eventually to Oklahoma. Somehow Granny stayed behind and set her home up out here in the hills."

"That's something I can't figure out," Kirsten said. "The land records say the forty acres is owned by somebody named Amelia Penn. I met Granny Gray Owl three or four times when I was trying to buy the place, and I rode out here to see if she could tell me how to contact Amelia Penn. Each time she told me to mind my own business—except the last time, about a month ago, when she said I could go to hell. She also called me a land-grabbing bitch. Foul mouthed old woman."

"Said the pot calling the kettle black."

Kirsten almost snapped back, but she didn't want to fuss with Thad tonight, and she knew he was probably irritated about her speaking ill of the dead. His underwear seemed to get cinched uptight about such things. It had been touchy between them lately, and she did not want to trigger a break—too much to sort out. Besides, she didn't have time to head back to the ranch after they returned to Medicine Wheel and hoped to get a bath at Thad's town place above the vet hospital. If she kept on good terms with him, maybe she could entice him into scrubbing her back and helping wash her hair. Then she'd do the same for him before she coaxed him into bed for a short spell.

After an awkward silence, Thad said, "I think we should put off any more searching. Sam should be here by sunrise, and that's his job. I'm going to see if I can get a few hours shuteye."

"I'm for that."

They peeled off their coats and spread them out on the springy tallgrass some distance from the lodge remnants. Before they could lie down and stretch out, Cinder began barking frantically from the direction of the canyon. Kirsten and Thad both turned and hurried toward the sound. Kirsten caressed the butt of her Colt but did not slip the weapon from its holster. When they arrived at the canyon's edge, Cinder ceased her barking and turned and looked up at them before she started down a deer trail that threaded among the trees and heavy undergrowth toward the canyon floor.

When they reached the bottom some ten minutes later, they stopped short of a shallow spring-fed stream that snaked along the point of the vee formed by the canyon walls. Cinder barked and took off again, racing easterly along the narrow streambank, leaving Kirsten nearly breathless as they stumbled along the rocky path. The Dalmatian disappeared, and they stopped to rest for a moment.

"What the hell's got into that dog?" Kirsten asked. "I thought she just chased fires."

"Or its victims," Thad replied.

"The victim's up the hill wrapped in a canvas tarp."

Thad shrugged and grinned back at her, "I love that you're such a patient woman."

"I don't love your sarcasm." Sometimes Thad's even-temperedness annoyed her. She tried to recall when she had seen him more than just a little miffed about something. He must have lost control sometime with somebody, but never with her, and she had certainly given him cause. He was the total opposite of the man she had married and subsequently shot. Thunderstorms of life swept over Thad like water off a duck's back. At least that's how it appeared. She wasn't sure she knew the real Thaddeus Jacob Locke. And that stood in the way of risking her heart enough to commit to a life with him. Lately, she wasn't certain how he now felt about the marriage proposal she had deflected with a brusque "have to think about that" several months ago. Things had changed after that.

They continued following the deer trail along the streambank, brushing back the over-hanging tree limbs and thorny bushes that were trying to overtake the path. It worried Kirsten that Cinder had been silent for some minutes, but Thad, of course, seemed unperturbed. Finally, the dog's frantic barking broke the eerie silence.

"She's stopped," Thad said, "and she's not far ahead."

Thad stepped up the pace, and Kirsten followed only a few steps behind. Soon she saw the Dalmatian's shadowy figure sitting on the trail ahead. She appeared to be nuzzling a dark creature hugged against her chest. The creature let forth a pitiful cry, like a child in distress. "What in the hell?"

"One of your lost goats—a kid," Thad said as he approached the waiting animals and knelt beside them, stroking Cinder's head with one hand and running his fingers through the baby goat's hair with the other. Cinder licked his face and then turned her attention back to the foundling. The kid bleated and snuggled against the dog.

Kirsten could see that the dog and kid had bonded. "She got separated from the herd and was left behind. Poor thing. We can't leave her here."

"Of course not. I'll have to carry her out."

"Can you do that?"

He stood and then picked up the kid and enfolded the goat in his arms. "About a thirty-pounder. I'll huff a bit going up the slope, but we'll make it." He slipped one hand between the kid's hind quarters, probing with his fingers. "A girl. She'll be a gorgeous nanny someday. Let's get this gal out of the canyon and then figure out what to do with her."

The kid was amazingly calm, Kirsten thought, as they trudged up the trail that led from the small canyon. She supposed that Cinder's presence was a major factor. Kirsten knew that the kid made an awkward load for Thad, but his heavily muscled arms and shoulders, the result of a profession that required wrestling cattle and horses daily, prepared him well for carrying such loads. He was also a six-footer with legs she teasingly called "gangle-shanked" that took long strides and moved his body along at a fair rate of speed.

When they reached the rim, he carried the kid to the grass in front of the former lodge and set her down. The kid bounced to Cinder and began nosing the Dalmatian's underside in search of a teat. Cinder looked up at Thad questioningly.

"Sorry, girl, you'll just have to tell her you can't help." He turned to Kirsten. "She'll be okay. She should be eating grass and grain by now. She's not totally weaned, though, and would be grabbing snacks from mom when she got the chance. Cute thing. It's too dark to tell for sure, but it looks like she's black with kind of a white moustache about her nose—white about her feet and ankles, too. Like socks." He hesitated a moment. "I think we should call her 'Socks.'"

"Don't name your livestock. Then they get to be family. That's tougher than hell when selling or butchering time comes."

"No way this gal's going to be sold or butchered. She's going to be Cinder's companion."

She shook her head in disbelief. "I'm going to plop down and snatch a few hours sleep. I'd welcome a companion."

Chapter 5

CINDER CLAIMED THAD'S canvas coat and settled on it with Socks snuggled up against her, and Thad inched between the new friends and Kirsten, securing a portion of each coat for his ground cover. Kirsten and the animals were asleep long before he finally closed his eyes. He awakened when he heard the blowing of horses and squeaking of wagon wheels approaching. He slipped out of the living wedge that had been formed by the creatures on each side of him and got up to greet the law.

Only a slender ribbon of light on the eastern horizon signaled the dawn of another day. Thad could barely make out the shadowy images of the wagon and two riders, but he was certain that the big bear of a man in one saddle was Sheriff Sam Mallery. He nudged Kirsten's booted foot with his. "Got company. Time to get up."

Cinder was already at his heels with Socks at the dog's side completing a duet of wagging tails, and the new friends followed him to greet the newcomers. The sheriff dismounted, followed by a slight, balding man, who was as small as Mallery was large. Dr. Horace Kleeb was a local physician who doubled as county coroner on the rare occasions the sheriff was required to investigate a suspicious death.

The doctor's credentials were dubious. Local gossip reported he drank to excess on occasion and tended to miss appointments, but he had his worshipers. Kleeb had shown up in Manhattan after the Civil War and set up shop as a physician. He claimed to have apprenticed in St. Louis before serving as a surgeon in the Union Army during the war. Thad concluded that meant the man was a self-ordained doctor, but that was not unusual before recent licensing laws were enacted. Unless there was a citizen complaint, nobody made a fuss over the qualifications of medical professionals engaged in practice prior to passage of the new regulations. Thad did not care. Wartime service and many years of private practice were probably worth more than his own two years of medical school.

Thad extended his hand to the Sheriff who responded with an iron grip. "Hello, Sam. Sorry to spoil your night's sleep."

"Goes with the job. Election's just a year off or I might have let you wait a spell."

He shook Kleeb's hand. "Good morning, doctor."

Kleeb replied with his high-pitched voice, "Where's the corpse? I've got patients to see today—live, human ones, who pay sooner than the county."

Thad could see that Kleeb's disposition had not improved any since their last encounter. He ignored the jab aimed at the species of Thad's patients and waved at George Stewart, a cherubic-faced, young deputy who sat on the wagon seat with the horses' reins clasped in his fingers. "Morning, George."

"Hi, Doc. Who are your friends?" He pointed to Cinder and the kid.

"Cinder's the mama. Her little one's name is Socks."

"You must have a story about them."

Doctor Kleeb cleared his throat and shot the deputy an annoyed look.

"Tell you about them later. We've got some business to take care of now," Thad said. He spoke to the Dalmatian. "Cinder. Stay." The dog sat, and Socks remained at her side. It occurred to Thad it would be interesting to attempt to train the goat.

He led the sheriff and coroner to the body. Fortunately, the sun had inched a bit higher and started to afford some light now, although Kirsten appeared out of the semi-darkness with a lighted kerosene lantern.

The sheriff looked at her in surprise and then rubbed his brushy, white moustache and smiled. "Why, Miss Cavelle. I ain't seen you for a spell."

"Not since I was a guest in your stinking excuse for a jail," she replied.

Mallery chuckled. "We were honored with your presence, ma'am."

"Thank you, but I don't plan on another visit any time soon."

Thad interrupted. "Over here, Sam." He pointed to the wrapped bundle and stepped toward it and knelt beside the body. He carefully folded back the tarp to expose the corpse.

The burly sheriff gagged and turned his head away. "Damn, Doc, you could have warned me."

Doctor Kleeb circled the body, but remained standing, looking at Granny's remains from a distance. "Very well," he said. "I would say she is dead. Is that all you got me out here for?"

Thad said, "You might want to look at her forehead. You would have to get a little closer."

Kleeb removed his hat and carried it over to the buckboard, where he also took off his waistcoat and tie, dropping everything on the wagon seat next to the deputy. As he returned, he rolled up his sleeves. "I will require some water and a cloth."

Kirsten quickly produced a canteen, and Thad pulled a handkerchief from his pocket. The coroner tugged the edge of the tarp out, so he could rest his knees on it and stiffly let himself down on the ground. He wet the kerchief with the canteen water and began wiping the blistered, baked flesh of the woman's forehead, probing the cavernous wound in her skull with his finger. He spoke to Thad, "Lift her right shoulder so I can twist the neck around and examine the remainder of the skull."

Thad complied, and Kleeb finished his examination. "Bullet wound, no doubt. No exit. Get her back to the county morgue, and I should be able find some lead, maybe make a guess on gun type, for all the good it will do." He tossed the canteen on the ground and handed Thad the filthy kerchief before he struggled upright with a hand from the sheriff.

The coroner limped over to the wagon. "I'm getting my things and heading back to Manhattan. Drop the old woman off at the morgue, and I'll get over there later and see what I can find."

After the coroner left, they placed Granny Gray Owl's body in the buckboard, and then Thad and Kirsten showed the sheriff around the scene. The sunrise offered full light now, so they were able to see the place outside the shroud of darkness for the first time.

"No tracks to speak of," the sheriff observed. "This limestone cover we got around here don't have any give to it, especially when it's been dry a few days. Wouldn't know anybody else had been around but for the bullet hole. George has been digging around in the rubble with your shovel and ain't turned up a gun, so it don't look like she done herself in. Besides, it'd be damned hard to shoot yourself between the eyes."

Thad said, "She didn't shoot herself, Sam. Questions are just who and why."

"Yup. Tell me about the goat."

Kirsten said, "She had a mule and a herd of goats. They're gone."

"Fire probably scared them off."

"She would have had them locked up for the night. Coyotes will take down goats, and even a cougar turns up occasionally. Too many night hazards in the hills for goats and small creatures," Kirsten said.

"So you think the killer rustled the critters? That don't make sense."

"I know," Kirsten said. "But we found this little gal at the bottom of the canyon by herself. Her mama wouldn't have gone off without her on purpose. I think the herd was being driven, and they got separated. The rustlers didn't miss the little one and pushed the nanny to go on with the herd."

"You been thinking about this, ain't you?"

"I have."

"Well, it's a theory, I guess. More than I got. But why would you kill an old woman and burn down her home just for a bunch of goats?"

"The goats were incidental."

Mallery cocked his head and looked at her suspiciously. "Incidental. Fancy word."

"The killer came for something else. Maybe he or she didn't find it and took the goats as a consolation prize. Or found it and took the goats as a bonus. Such a person would not be beyond greed."

"You said 'he or she.' Are you saying a woman could have done this?"

"Women kill."

He shook his head. "Guess you ought to know. But a woman didn't do this. Kill somebody and take off with a goat herd."

"Maybe there was more than one."

"You're getting this damned complicated. How long have you been a lawman?"

"Never. But maybe it's time for a new sheriff in Riley County. I might run myself."

"You're a woman. The voters wouldn't elect no female."

"You're forgetting, Sam. The legislature just passed a bill giving women the right to vote in local elections. I'm betting I could collect a fair amount of these new voters. And the women would get their husbands to sign on or find another place to sleep."

"You a Democrat? Voters here would vote for a skunk before they'd vote for a Democrat."

"I'm nothing. They're all a bunch of unprincipled thieves. I would get signatures and get on the ballot by petition."

Thad could see Sam was seriously pondering her words and decided to cut off a fuss that was turning nasty. "If we find the goats, I know how to identify them as Granny's."

The others both looked at him incredulously. Kirsten snapped, "Who gives a shit? That's not what we were talking about."

"That's what we should be talking about if we want to find Granny's killer." He pointed to Socks, standing next to Cinder. "Two notches at the top of the left ear. I'll bet every goat in the herd was notched that way. Proves your ownership. Some cattlemen do that right after a calf is born. They have their own notch code and avoid branding. More humane."

"Oh God. Humane. Next, you'll be wanting to do that to our Red Angus herd."

"I've thought about it."

"A cold day in hell."

"Let's get back to finding Granny's killer. Sam, don't you think somebody ought to try to track those goats?"

"Through that canyon? Rock and water. Never find them."

"They'll leave droppings some place."

"I ain't doing nothing that can't be done from horseback. And George has got to get Granny back to town before she gets to stinking. Maybe I'll send him out tomorrow or the next day."

"You know, Sam, there could be a motive here. I've heard folks speculate for years about Granny having money hid on her place. I know for a fact she charged a good price for her remedies, and she obviously never spent much of it."

That seemed to pique the sheriff's interest. "You don't say? Maybe we'll come back with a crew and look around. For now, I'm headed back to town. You can untie your mounts from the back of the wagon. George, I can't wait for you. Just check in when you get back to town." He wheeled and ambled toward his horse.

Kirsten called after him. "See you on election day, Sheriff."

Thad chided her, "Was that necessary?"

"I'm just joshing him. Maybe. Could I take a bath at your place?"

"Yeah. But I need one, too. Need to get this smoke smell off."

"You wash my back, and I'll wash yours."

Chapter 6

I T WAS JUST a few minutes past seven thirty in the morning when Myles Locke opened the single window in his office to catch some breeze and slipped off his waistcoat and hung it on the wall peg next to his chair. No sooner had he eased his lanky frame into the swivel chair behind his desk than someone tapped softly on the closed door. He knew it was Serena Belmont because she would be the only other occupant of the Locke & Locke offices at this early hour. His son, Cameron, would not arrive from his ranch northeast of Manhattan before nine o'clock when the two clerks came on duty.

"Come in, Serena," he said. "You don't have to knock." But she always did.

Serena stepped in with the perky smile that never failed to brighten his day, a perfect tonic for an old man who had recently crossed the bridge to his seventies. As usual, she was impeccably and professionally attired. Her heritage was a melting pot of Irish, Seneca and African, her flawless skin the color of burnt sienna. The petite young woman just shy of her thirtieth birthday was even smarter than she was beautiful, and that was saying something.

"Good morning, Judge," Serena said. "Can your spare me a few minutes?"

"Of course. Take a chair. Something I can help you with?"

Serena sat down, and her face turned serious. "I have had an opportunity presented to me, and I don't want to accept it without your approval."

Myles felt a moment of apprehension. He hoped she was not about to announce departure from the firm. She had carved herself a vital niche as a lawyer in the office. He and Cam expected to offer her a full partnership in another year. "You don't require my approval to pursue any opportunity, Serena, but you have certainly commanded my attention."

"As you know, since I've returned to Manhattan I have continued to serve as general counsel for the Bill of Rights Society."

"Yes. And the fees have been a nice contribution to firm revenues. Those folks obviously thought highly of you after working full-time for them for five or six years."

"I did the legal work to set up the organization, so I really had an advantage over anyone else who might have wanted the job. I love working for them. I believe in their efforts to preserve individual liberty, and I enjoy being paid to take the train to the capital city to visit old friends two or three times a year. But they have an interesting and challenging temporary job they would like to have me take on now."

"I like the sound of 'temporary.'"

"It would require a three- to four-month leave of absence from the firm. The board of directors would like to employ me to travel from coast to coast to train other lawyers to handle cases on behalf of the society so they could represent either defendants or plaintiffs where Bill of Rights issues are a concern. During my travels I would be assigned speaking engagements planned to give the organization a greater national profile and, hopefully encourage donations."

Myles breathed more easily. She was not leaving the firm. "I would certainly be agreeable to that."

"My expenses would be paid, and the fees are well above the salary I'm receiving here. I would expect the fees to be paid to the firm and the gross to be added to my billings for purposes of calculating my year-end bonus. We should all make money from the endeavor. I just wouldn't be available to handle my usual case load. That wouldn't affect you much because I don't do significant real estate and probate-type work."

"Cam's had it too easy since you joined the firm anyway. He'll just have to spend less time with his cows for a few months. You haven't spoken with him about this?"

"No. You're senior partner. I wasn't going to bother him with it if I didn't obtain your approval first."

"Well, you have my approval. Do you want me to discuss it with Cam?"

"No. That's my responsibility. I'll speak with him when he gets to the office. I checked his calendar, and it's clear this morning."

"May I ask a family question?"

"Certainly."

"What about Ned during this time?"

"If Cam is okay with my plans, I will speak to Thad. Ned's been with Thad off and on most of the summer anyway, and I know he'd be thrilled to stay with him while I'm gone. He would need to enroll at the Medicine Wheel school for a semester, I suppose."

"You know as well as I do that Thad will be delighted to have him."

"Yes, I didn't worry a second about that. He is a truly good man. I'll never forgive myself for what I did to him."

"What's done is done, Serena. Don't be so hard on yourself. What counts is what we do going forward." Now if he could just convince himself of the truth of his own words. He continued, "Most of us need healthy measures of forgiveness along life's trail. I sure have. And I know Thad has forgiven you. Grudges are not a part of his make-up."

Serena got up, quickly skirted around the desk and bent over and gave Myles a soft peck on the cheek. "Thad isn't a better man than his father, though. Thanks, Judge. For everything."

Myles watched as she disappeared through the door and was struck by a wave of sadness that things had not worked out differently for Thad and Serena. Ned was their son from a teenage summer romance. Serena was the daughter of J. Quincy and Rachael Belmont, who operated a large hog farm and meat processing enterprise in the Medicine Wheel area. Serena had resided in Washington, D. C. with an aunt and attended school there and had been visiting her parents for the summer. She returned to school after learning of her pregnancy, gave birth to her baby boy there, and never informed Thad. He only learned of the child nearly ten years later when Serena returned to Riley County on a visit and ended up representing Kirsten Cavelle against murder charges arising out of her husband's death. He finally met his son when Serena returned to the Flint Hills to join the firm. Thad and Serena had since taken different paths, however, and their reunion was not a fairy tale ending. The two were civil, though, and Serena encouraged Thad's relationship with his newly discovered son.

Myles combed his fingers through his thick white hair, sighed and reached for the top file folder on the stack on his desktop. He was a man who sought order and predictability. He found those things only in the sanctuary of his office. He supposed that was why he lived so much of his life there.

By the time he heard the familiar rattle of file drawers and typewriters and footsteps in the outer offices, Myles had handwritten two wills and a farm purchase contract. He started to get up to take the parchment sheets to Reva Duncan for editing and typing when his right arm opened the door and walked in. His and Reva's relationship had passed the knocking stage quickly after she took over the office almost thirty years ago while a pregnant teenager. She had married the impregnator,

Carl Duncan, and borne four more children for him during brief maternity breaks from the office. Carl was a day laborer who worked when his back or knee or something else didn't hurt, which was only occasional. Myles supposed ladies would see the man as a handsome devil, but it was otherwise difficult to understand why the still attractive Reva put up with the lout.

"Good morning, Reva. I've got some work for you. I was just going to bring it out." She marched up to his desk and snatched the papers from his hand and sat down.

"And I've got some news for you."

He leaned back in his chair and rubbed his chin to signal his impatience. "When do I get to hear this news?"

"Well, I ran into Mabel just as I got outside the office door. You know her. She does the sheriff's paperwork several days a week."

"Yes, the one with the mouth that cannot keep secrets."

"That's not kind. Mabel has been a valuable source of information for the firm over the past ten years."

"Why don't you just give me the news?"

"Granny Gray Owl is dead."

It was difficult to maintain his normally stoic demeanor, but he betrayed no emotion and stared at his clerk-office honcho with his steel-gray eyes for several moments before responding. "And how does your friend Mabel know this to be a fact?"

"Don't play 'Mister Calm' with me. You're shocked. I can tell. Mabel had gone into the Sheriff's office early to get some work done while it was quiet. Sam came in. He had just been out to Granny's. Somebody burned her place down, but they apparently shot her first. George is bringing the body to town in a buckboard."

"Murdered? I can't imagine why anyone would kill that little old lady. She never harmed a soul in her life."

"You could probably say that about most folks who get murdered."

He pushed his chair back and stood up, plucked his coat from its peg and tugged it on. "I'm going to visit the Sheriff's office and try to find out what happened."

"I'll dig out the Amelia Penn files and leave them on your desk."

Chapter 7

SHERIFF SAM MALLERY did not open his eyes when Myles walked into the office. Leaning back in his chair with booted feet propped up on his desk, Sam appeared to be napping. Myles quietly pulled back the chair in front of the desk and sat down.

"What in the hell do you want, Myles?" Mallery growled, not bothering to open his eyes or lift his feet off the desk. They were longtime contemporaries and did not bother with formalities.

"I stopped by to ask about Granny Gray Owl."

"Where did you hear about Granny? We ain't even got the body back to town yet."

"Confidential."

"I suppose Reva got Mabel flapping her lips again. I ought to fire the old heifer for talking too much."

"Do you really want to take on the paperwork your-self?"

The sheriff pushed his chair back and slid his feet off the desktop.

"She's got me by the balls, don't she?"

"I would say so."

"So, what do you want to know about Granny? I can't tell you much. Confidential."

He knew Mallery would have to strike back. Time to make peace. "Perhaps we can trade information that will make life easier for both of us."

"What do you got to trade?"

"I know Granny's real name. That might be helpful for your reports."

"She's not Gray Owl?"

"She's not even Kaw—or any other Indian for that matter."

Myles had the sheriff's attention now. "Tell me about her and why you even have any interest in Granny's case."

"Granny's real name is Amelia Penn. I drafted her will, and I expect to be named executor of her estate within the next few weeks. I can't discuss the contents of her will until it is filed with the probate court and becomes a public record."

"I see. Well, I guess that makes you the person I talk to about Granny. Does she have any family we should contact?"

"A grandnephew, Thomas Penn."

"Not Gray Owl, neither. Where does all this Indian stuff come from?"

"Granny's brother married a Kaw, so their son was a half blood. He married a half-blood, so Thomas is a half blood, too."

"This is confusing me. I don't give a damn how much Kaw anybody's got."

"Well, just for your education, there are less than two hundred full blood Kaw surviving, mostly on the reservation in Oklahoma. But back to the nephew. I have a St. Louis address for him. He's an architect. I can send him a telegram, if you like."

"I would take that kindly. When Doc Kleeb's done with the body, he'll need to know where she goes. What do I tell him?"

"I'll make arrangements with Harley Richardson. Tell him to notify Harley."

"I'll do that." Mallery sighed heavily. "With election just a year off, I sure as hell didn't need a murder on my plate."

"Look at the positive side. Solve it, and you'll be a hero."

"And if I don't, I'll be a goat. Speaking of which—"

"Yes."

"Granny's goats run off. And her mule, too. Crazy Kirsten thinks the killer rustled them."

"Let me tell you something, Sam. Nobody in Riley County is smarter than Kirsten Cavelle—man or woman. Only a fool doesn't listen carefully to what Kirsten has to say. And I would hate to think you were a fool."

"Well, I had been planning to send my deputy out to see if he can track the goats after he gets in town with the corpse."

"I figured you would be on top of things, Sam."

Chapter 8

AFTER RETURNING TO his office Myles asked Reva to send a telegram to Thomas Penn about Granny's death. "Don't mention the murder. I would rather discuss that face-to-face. I'm certain he will make train connections and be here in a few days. We sent him a letter a year ago about Granny's requested burial arrangements. She wants to be buried on her land. I'll go over the details with you later since there will be a few people we need to contact."

"I doubt if 'we' are going to be doing this. I'm betting Reva will be contacting these folks."

"You just won your bet. Thank you, Reva. I do appreciate all you do."

Myles knew that Reva would take care of all the details and that she would have scolded him for not delegating the work if he had not assigned it to her. It was just a game they played. After Reva left the office, he turned to the file folders she had placed in a small pile on his desk. He opened the top file and found an envelope sealed with wax and emblazoned with the words "Last Will and Testament of Amelia Penn." He considered opening it and then decided to wait. He had a carbon copy in the file for reference and decided to wait until he met with Granny's nephew. Some folks liked a little formality with a will's opening, although it was legally unnecessary.

It was a simple document. He crusaded for simplicity in legal documents, generally to no avail. He occasionally complained that some lawyers charged by the pound for their words, motivating them to produce incomprehensible contracts, wills, and other official papers. The client was, of course, expected to sign in reliance upon the lawyer's translation of the gibberish.

Granny's will left the forty-acre tract where her former lodge had been located to her grandnephew, Thomas Penn. There was a strange bequest to Thaddeus Locke of "the contents of the can located in the goat pen," and the residue of the estate was to go to a trust to be established by the will's executor for educating Kansa—locally known as Kaw—Indians of at least one-quarter blood. Myles Locke was named executor of the will and trustee of the trust. In the event of his death or incapacity,

Thaddeus Locke was named successor. Since Thad was not a lawyer, Myles had found Granny's designation of Thad a bit strange, but his job was to carry out his client's wishes, and there was no legal requirement that a lawyer serve as executor.

He was especially baffled by the bequest to his son, Thad. Granny had remained tight-lipped about it and said simply it would all become self-evident. A can in a goat pen? Like a pot of gold, perhaps?

He opened the folder that had been removed with the will from the office safe and sorted through the bundle of stock certificates he found there: Wells Fargo & Co., an established banking and express firm; Union Pacific Railway and a half dozen smaller regional railroad stocks; Rockefeller's Standard Oil Company and several wildcat oil companies with operations in Oklahoma Territory and Texas, of all places. The "wildcatter" searched for oil in unproven areas. The term had long been used as slang for risky business ventures, and Myles thought he would ordinarily dispose of such stocks, but the will mandated that no stock be sold until at least ten years following the death of Amelia Penn. In the meantime, only dividends could be used to fund the educational trust.

He had been Granny's lawyer for nearly thirty years and had acted as her agent under power of attorney to make her stock purchases on the New York Stock Exchange, but she had never once asked for his investment advice. And he did not offer. What did he know, a country lawyer who held not a single share of stock? He had arranged for monthly delivery of investment bulletins published by Dow Jones & Company and other financial information to her lodge. The investment publishing firm had been established by Charles Henry Dow and several associates a half dozen years earlier, and Granny had instructed Myles to purchase a subscription to a new publication, The Wall Street Journal, planned by the Dow firm, as soon as it became available.

He reviewed his file notes and saw that the market value of Granny's investments had been just short of two hundred thousand dollars when he last checked a few months ago. In terms of wealth that would have placed her in the top two or three of Riley County's residents. Tongues would start wagging when he completed an inventory and filed it with the probate court and her assets became a public record.

It suddenly occurred to him that he should visit the scene of Granny's death. He was responsible for the property until it was transferred to the nephew some months hence, and he had never visited the woman's residence. She had always insisted on coming to the office. Perhaps he could speak with Thad while he was near Medicine Wheel. He decided to see if he could join Deputy Stewart on his investigation at Granny's place. Myles doubted if he could find the burned-out lodge on his own.

He put the will and stock certificates back in the safe and plucked his hat from the antler hanger on the wall and informed Reva of his plans before heading back to the sheriff's office.

Chapter 9

MYLES RARELY RODE a horse these days, but a buggy would have taken too much time. It was nearly noon, and Deputy George Stewart wanted to get out to the crime scene, complete what he obviously considered a futile effort to track the goats, and return to Manhattan before dark. Myles just wanted to check the goat pen.

His skinny butt and inner thighs were sore and tender by the time the riders approached Medicine Wheel. His lower back took a shock of pain with every saddle bounce. He wondered now about the wisdom of the journey. He surrendered a resigned smile at the thought Vedette might pamper him when he returned home, especially if he dropped a groan or two. Vedette Joliet had been his companion and lover of some twenty-five years. An exotic, olive-skinned woman of mixed Negro, French,

Spanish, English and Cherokee blood, Vedette's roots lay in Louisiana where her parents had been free Negroes. After her mother's death during the War of the Rebellion, she had escaped to Kansas, a free state where her status would not be challenged.

The deputy interrupted Myles's dream world, to which he knew he had a bad habit of escaping. "Judge, do you still want to stop off and see if your son's in town?"

"Yes, George, if you don't mind. It won't take but a few minutes."

"Fine by me. Them goat tracks ain't going any place."

They rode into Medicine Wheel, and Myles dismounted and hitched his sorrel gelding at the rail in front of Thad's vet clinic. He paused a moment when he glanced at the fire hall across the street and saw a big spotted dog sitting in front of the building, licking what appeared to be a baby goat.

"Do you see that?" he asked Stewart.

"Dog's called 'Cinder.' The kid's 'Socks.' When the goats got herded off, the kid got left behind. Cinder found her and adopted the little gal, I guess."

Myles shrugged and walked into the clinic. There was no one in the receiving area, so he called, "Thad."

"Back here in the surgery, Dad. Come on back. I'm just finishing up."

He took a few steps down a short hallway and peered in an open doorway. There he saw his son with bloodied fingers cleaning up a wound at the base of a big, orange tabby cat's tail. An obviously anxious, middle-aged lady with wisps of white and black hair dropping over her forehead leaned over the table, anchoring the yowling animal's front and hind legs with an iron grip.

"You can let go of the legs, Mary. But keep the big guy on the table. I have some powder to put on the wound." He found a little leather bag with a drawstring, opened it, and shook some of the gray, powdery contents on the wicked-looking open wound. He handed the bag to the woman, who looked at him questioningly.

"Sprinkle this on the wound once a day. It should help with the healing. I can't sew it up. We've got to let it drain. I think we can save his tail, but if it starts to swell again, bring him back."

"Thank you, Doctor. If it's okay, I'll stop in each week to pay you something. Or could I pay you with fresh eggs?"

"Eggs would be fine, Mary."

"Please don't send a bill. Herman would be furious with my spending money on a cat, but Oscar is my best friend."

"I understand, Mary. Your secret's safe with me."

Myles stepped aside as the woman departed the surgery with the tomcat tucked in her arms. Thad turned toward his father as he wiped the bloody, putrid-smelling mess off the table. "Hi, Dad. What are you doing in Medicine Wheel?"

Myles stepped into the room and approached his son. "I'm going out to Granny Gray Owl's place with the deputy. I will be executor for her estate. There's something I want to search for. I was wondering if you might like to join me?"

"Sorry, Dad. I have an appointment at the Carlton ranch to dehorn a troublemaking bull. I was out to Granny's place last night with the fire brigade. The lodge was pretty much burned out. I don't think there's anything left to find. That little bag of powder I gave to Mary was one of Granny's concoctions. I'm going to miss her in my practice. I was probably her best customer. She didn't sell cheap, but her Kaw medicines and remedies were worth the price. I considered her a good friend."

"She must have felt the same about you. She appointed you an alternate executor and trustee in her will. You don't have any immediate responsibilities, but I would like to have you stop by the office and discuss her arrangements the next time you're in Manhattan."

"I'll do that as soon as I can, Dad."

"Good. Now I'm going to visit Granny's goat pen."

"Why?"

"I'll tell you about it when you come into the office."

"That's one way to get me in soon."

Chapter 10

AS THEY APPROACHED Granny's ravaged building site, Deputy Stewart said, "Judge, can you use that rifle in your saddle holster?"

"It's been a good spell, but, yes. Why?"

Stewart signaled Myles to halt and reined in his own horse. "Somebody's scavenging through the lodge rubble. Looks like two of them. Don't see no horses. Must have come up from the canyon. Better ride in slow and careful-like."

Myles's fingers brushed the stock of his Winchester. He had never fired a gun at a man, much less killed one, and the prospect of doing either made him uneasy. With reservations he nudged his gelding forward at a slow pace, following the deputy toward Granny's burned-out lodge. He saw the scavengers now, two of them, one a big, bearish man, the other appearing younger and looking like a walking scarecrow. He hoped they were just a pair of looters who were not looking for a confrontation.

Myles gave a sigh of relief when the interlopers evidently sighted the newcomers and began to run in the direction of the canyon. Stewart spurred his horse forward to give chase, leaving Myles to swallow his dust. The lawyer then eased the reins on his own horse and urged it ahead. By the time he reached the lodge, however, the deputy had disappeared over the canyon's rim. He dismounted and hitched his horse to a low-hanging branch of a mulberry tree near what he assumed was the goat pen, noticing that Stewart's mount was grazing unfettered in the nearby tallgrass. He yanked his rifle from its scabbard and hesitated, debating whether to wait or to try to locate George Stewart. Against his better judgment, he decided to head into the canyon.

Myles rushed past the charred remnants of the lodge and began pacing the canyon's edge until he found the trampled grass and broken limbs that signaled a pathway. He broke through the gap in the brush and walked tentatively down the twisting deer trail that obviously led to the canyon floor. Because of the thickness of the gnarled oak trees and undergrowth, he could not see far ahead, and the tree branches whipped and clawed his face, tossing off his hat repeatedly. He found the rough trail with its ragged hurdles of protruding limestone tricky-going, and he stumbled, tumbling forward and landing on the ungiving stone and dropping the Winchester.

As he righted himself and picked up his rifle, the unmistakable crack of gunfire broke out in the direction of the canyon floor. He could not pinpoint the location because of the echoes off the steep canyon banks, but he did not hesitate and resumed his journey down the incline as fast as he could move. As he crashed through the brush and reached the canyon floor and the tiny stream that flowed there, the guns silenced. Myles readied his rifle and looked up and down the stream, searching for George Stewart. At first, he could find no sign of the deputy, and then he caught a glimpse of booted feet sticking out of some overhanging brush and blocking the stream's flow, water swirling around and leaping over the obstructions.

Myles walked hesitantly along the stream's edge. He knew what he was going to find but felt duty-bound to confirm. His eyes scanned the tree-covered slopes that rose from the canyon floor, but his untrained eyes saw nothing threatening. He hoped the scavengers had continued their retreat. When he reached the brush that hid the owner of the boots, he pulled back a clump of the undergrowth and revealed the deputy's bloodied body. He was obviously dead with several wounds torn into his torso in addition to the ugly hole in his temple.

There was nothing he could do here. He needed to return to Medicine Wheel and alert Thad to the situation here. Then he would ride to Manhattan and inform the sheriff of the death of his deputy. He turned to start his climb back to the canyon's rim, but his path was sealed off by a black-bearded giant with a wicked grin displaying broken, rotting teeth and gaping holes. Clutched in his hands was a rifle that Myles thought was large enough to bring down an elephant.

"Who are you?" the big man asked.

"I might ask the same of you, mister." Myles knew his response was not prudent, but he was angry and that smothered his fear. Besides, now he had seen the skinny young man up the slope and off to his left side with the rifle aimed at him. His chances of walking out of the canyon were no better than that of a mouse caught in a bull snake's jaws.

"Smart mouth, huh. Well, I thought you looked familiar. Now I remember. I seen you at the courthouse with a fancy-looking nigger woman. My friend said you was both law wranglers. Your name's Locke."

Myles slowly started to raise his Winchester to hip level, hoping he might squeeze the trigger and get off a shot at the oaf. The obstructer made an ample target. But he was too late. The man had already taken a step toward him, and the rifle butt was driving like a sledge toward his head. He started to duck away, but his effort was futile, and he was hardly aware of it when the weapon drove into the side of his skull and knocked him immediately senseless.

Chapter 11

VEDETTE JOLIET OBSESSIVELY pulled back the curtains and looked out and then returned to her rocking chair for a few moments before she got up again and went to the window. She was watching for Myles to stroll up the stone front walk to the covered porch. He had stopped by the house to warn her he might be a bit tardy because of his visit to Granny Gray Owl's house. He was a man of routine, very predictable in his habits by those who knew him well. And no person knew Myles Locke better than Vedette. Ordinarily he would walk through the door within five minutes on either side of six o'clock, greatly simplifying her supper plans. Six o'clock had passed several hours earlier, although a star-lit sky made the night less foreboding.

Again she sat back down on the cushioned rocker next to the table on which a large kerosene lamp cast a healthy glow in the parlor. She had set the flame high to provide ample reading light for the twelve-year-old boy who sat on the other side of the table in his grandfather's favorite chair, hypnotized by the latest book that had captured his interest. Ned Locke's presence was calming, perhaps the only thing preserving her sanity this evening. Serena was arguing a case before the Kansas Supreme Court in Topeka tomorrow and had boarded a train for the capital city some fifty miles east after the Locke office closed for the day. Vedette had gladly offered to take her son until Serena returned in two days. She got up and went to the window again.

"What's the matter, Grandma? Are you worried about Gramps?"

She turned back to Ned. Certainly he would have noticed her agitation. He didn't miss much. She savored being called "Grandma," grateful that the unfailingly kind Serena had so anointed her. She was related to the boy by neither blood nor marriage, although she could change this in an instant by accepting a marriage proposal that would likely be coming from Myles again soon. She had put him off for a bit more than twenty-five years now, the first proposal arriving on her thirtieth birthday. She thought her African blood, though diluted to triviality, brought too many problems to such a union, notwithstanding that Kansas had no laws imposing racial restrictions on marital unions.

"Yes, I am concerned," she replied to the boy with flawless almond-colored skin who shared her racial dilemma. Neither white nor Negro, looked upon with suspicion in both worlds, although, for a reason she never understood, she could choose to call herself Negro but did not have the option to be white, even though more of her heritage was European. Perhaps, another generation away from slavery, the nation would become colorblind, and it would make no difference.

Ned put his book aside, eased out of the chair and walked over to her side and gently wrapped his arm about her shoulders. He was just a gangly boy, but she thought of him as a man-child he was so mature and sensitive beyond his years. She slipped away and faced him and grasped his shoulders, fastening her eyes on his. It was then she realized it. "My Lord, Ned, when did this happen? You're taller than I am now, and I stand a strong five and a half feet."

Ned grinned and shrugged. "I don't know. I passed Mom over a year ago." He hesitated. "Grandma, it's almost nine o'clock. Why don't I run down to the livery and see if Gramps has turned his horse in? Maybe he stopped at the office. I can check there."

"I don't like having you run around in the dark." She thought for a moment she might join him, but she wanted to be home in case Myles showed up.

"The gas street lamps light up the downtown, and I can outrun any troublemaker in this town. I won't take long. I'll come right back with word."

He raced out the door before she could protest further.

The next half hour seemed like a day, but finally Vedette peered between the curtains and saw a shadowy form racing up the street toward the house. She opened the door to greet Ned, who stepped into the hallway. He was breathing heavily so she gave him a moment while they walked into the parlor.

He did not wait for her questions. "Gramps didn't show up with the rent horse. Deputy Stewart stables his work mount there, too. And he didn't bring his horse in either."

"I don't like what I am hearing."

"I saw a light at the sheriff's office and stopped there. Sheriff Sam was inside talking with Deputy Heinz. I asked him about Gramps and Deputy Stewart, and he said he wasn't worried about them—that he figured it got late and they decided to stay over in Medicine Wheel.

He said Gramps was probably at Dad's place and Deputy Stewart likely bunked on a hay pile in the fire hall."

"Your grandfather knows I would be very worried. If his horse went lame, he would have rented another in Medicine Wheel or borrowed one from your father. There are good roads between here and there. Starlight is good tonight. Tell me something."

"Yes, ma'am."

"Do you think the sheriff was telling the truth when he said he wasn't worried?"

"No, ma'am. I don't."

"Could you ride that Appaloosa mare of yours out to your dad's at sunrise and let him know Gramps went out to Granny's and hasn't come back? Do you think he'd be at Medicine Wheel or his ranch house?"

"I'll pick up Primrose at the livery first thing. Dad's in Medicine Wheel most days even if he's spent the night at the ranch. He's so busy doctoring critters, he usually only gets to the ranch when I'm with him. His only full-time hand, Jed Scott, pretty much runs the place—with Miss Kirsten stopping by to check up on him from time to time. She's pretty bossy, you know?"

"Is that right?" Vedette knew Kirsten and her reputation.

"Yeah. But I like her a lot."

"So do I."

Chapter 12

THAD WAS AWAKENED by persistent rapping on the clinic door downstairs. He sat up and swung his feet off the bed. He scolded himself. The sun had been up an hour, and he should have had his day started by now. He reached over to tap Kirsten on her rear but hit empty space. He looked over his shoulder and saw that her side of the bed was vacant. She must have got up earlier and headed for her ranch. He was not surprised. They rarely woke up together these days, and he missed that. But last night she slept part of the night with him. Lately, after she had had her way, she tended to just quickly get dressed and leave without so much as a peck goodbye. Kirsten had bewildered him with visits the past two nights. He had a feeling she wanted to talk about something, but could not, which was not like her at all.

He got up and slipped into his shirt and britches and hurried down the steep stairway, picking up a splinter in his bare foot. The stairway opened onto a short hallway that led into his reception area. He stopped, and, standing on a single foot, plucked the splinter from the other before crossing the room, flipping the bolt lock and opening the exterior door. He was surprised to find his son standing there with his Appaloosa mare hitched to the rail behind him. "Ned, come in. What are you doing here so early?"

"It's about Gramps."

A wave of apprehension struck his stomach. "What do you mean?"

"He didn't come home last night. He was headed out to Granny Gray Owl's with Deputy Stewart. I talked to Sheriff Sam. The deputy didn't come back either. Grandma hoped Gramps stopped by and stayed over at your place."

"No. But he stopped here on his way out there. That was early afternoon." He put his arm around Ned's shoulder. "Come on upstairs. I'll finish getting dressed while we talk. I've got some sweet rolls I picked up at Maudie's Bake Shoppe a few days ago. They're still more than edible. I'm guessing you haven't had breakfast."

"Nope. I left while it was still dark. Grandma didn't like it much, but we weren't sleeping. Why waste more time? Of course, where sweet rolls are concerned, I'll eat those anytime."

The upstairs space consisted of three rooms, a small parlor, and a tiny kitchen and a bedroom. The stairway opened onto the parlor, and Thad gestured to the kitchen. "Rolls are on the kitchen table in the sack. Help yourself. I'll be with you in a minute."

After he pulled on his socks and boots, Thad joined Ned in the kitchen. He was pleased to find hot coals still glowed in the woodstove and that Kirsten had left a simmering pot of coffee on the stove. She must not have beat him out of bed by too much. And ornery as she could be, she had a gentle, thoughtful side that most folks never saw. She might argue and debate with him, and she could be headstrong, but they had never attacked each other personally, verbally or otherwise, and he had never found a speck of meanness or pettiness in her.

He poured a tin mug full of coffee, sat down and snatched a roll before Ned ate them all. "Ned, you talked to the sheriff. When was that?"

Ned licked the maple-flavored frosting off his fingers and replied. "Last night when I went to the livery to see if Gramps had returned his rent-horse. He said he would look into things this morning if Gramps and Deputy Stewart didn't show up. I don't think he will hurry."

The boy had Sam figured out. The sheriff didn't know the meaning of hurry. "I'm going to ride out to Granny's now and see if I can find any sign of them. Maybe a horse went lame, and they had to stay the night."

"Can I go with you?"

He could see the excitement in Ned's eyes, and he hated to disappoint him, but he had no idea what he might find, and he feared it might be something a boy should not have to witness. "No. You need to get back to Manhattan and tell your grandma you found me and that I'm on my way to Granny's. Before you leave Medicine Wheel, though, I would like to have you see if you can find Kirsten at the livery or the company office. If she's in town, tell her what you told me and that I've left for Granny's."

Ned's face was downcast, but he was unusually mature and responsible for his age, and Thad knew there would be no protest or whining. He credited Serena for that.

"Her blue roan gelding was hitched outside the company office when I rode down Main Street."

Thad figured she must have stopped at her town office before heading out to her ranch. "If you can't catch her there, just ride back to Manhattan. If you meet the sheriff, tell him I'll meet him at Granny's. Tell your grandma I will ride into Manhattan and come to her place just as soon as I know something—or get word to her."

Thad pushed back his chair and got up from the table. He reached up and grabbed his Winchester from the rack above the entryway door, snatching his hat off the wall peg as he started for the stairway. Ned followed him down the stairs, and the instant they stepped outside the clinic, ran for his horse and gracefully stepped into the mare's saddle. Thad envied his son's ease on horseback. He certainly did not pick up that skill from his father. His brother, Cam, and Kirsten constantly offered riding tips to Thad to no avail. His vocation forced a lot of time on horseback, but he was the first to admit his horsemanship was nothing fancy. Kirsten had probably coached Ned more than anybody.

He watched Ned and Primrose disappear in a swirling cloud of dust and then hurried around the corner of his clinic toward the rear of the structure where he maintained a small stable for occasional patients and his own mount. He, too, rode an Appaloosa, a gelding. Cam was the premiere Appaloosa breeder in Kansas and would have taken it as an insult if Thad took up with outside stock. Besides, Thad's first horse, Cato, who now lived in semi-retirement at his owner's ranch, had been a gift from Cam.

Thad saddled the young horse that he called Inkblot, so named because of the irregular black patch of hair that covered nearly one side of its face and that flowed half way down its neck. It appeared more ink had been splattered on the underlying white of the hips and rump. Thad had selected the horse because he liked its color, and Inkblot was a truly gentle, almost docile creature in sharp contrast with the spirited animals Kirsten and Cam preferred.

He decided he would take Cinder with him. She was not a bloodhound, but she had a good nose. He led the Appaloosa across the street to the fire hall where Cinder sat watching his approach eagerly and wagging her tail while Socks slept snuggled up to the dog's hip. He released the horse's reins, stepped over to Cinder and her ward and scratched the Dalmatian's ears before bending over and lifting the startled kid into his arms. The kid began bleating frantically, and Cinder followed, whimpering with concern, as Thad carried the young goat back across the street to the clinic where he deposited the anxious creature in a large dog cage in the rear of the building. While Cinder stayed behind to reassure the kid, he went out the backdoor to the stable, where he pumped a bucket of water and gathered up an armload of hay and carried it to the goat's cage. The kid was not the least pacified, but he could not have her traipsing along behind Cinder. The dog had work to do.

Kirsten was waiting at the fire hall when he returned.

"Ned caught me just as I was heading out to the ranch," she said. "I'm going with you."

"You don't have to if you've got things to do."

"I know."

Chapter 13

UNBURDENED BY WAGONS, Thad figured his usual shortcut to Granny's place would take half an hour. Kirsten, of course, knew a route that shaved off ten minutes. It was still early morning, but the sun's warming rays had already sneaked over the Flint Hills enough to suck a light dew off the tallgrass that swished against their horses' bellies as they approached the ruins. Cinder was hidden in the grass but for the waves of its parting as she rushed ahead of the riders.

"This grass needs to be grazed down," Kirsten said.

"By Red Angus cows, I assume."

"Why not? We've got part of our herd grazing the grass on my land that adjoins this. We'd just put in a gate between the places. Repair some of the fence Granny had let run down."

He knew she was trying to distract him from the thoughts that were racing through his mind. They had bought a half section of land together several years earlier, but he had owned a small Hereford herd, and Kirsten had a Red Angus herd triple the size of his. She was dead-set on building a purebred herd that would have no equal. She had persuaded him to sell the Herefords, borrow a bit of money, and partner with her in the Red Angus business. Red Angus herds were uncommon. He knew of no other in Kansas, and their best purebred market was further east in Missouri and Kentucky. Their bulls were sold everywhere for cross-breeding, however. Kirsten managed the operation, and they were making money he never saw because profits went into buying more cattle. He was involved in lesser ways with others of Kirsten's ventures, including Medicine Wheel, and he worried some about what would happen if they had a personal falling out. It could be like a divorce without marriage, he feared.

"Thad," Kirsten said. "Off to the right. Riderless horse."

He turned Inkblot in the direction of the bay that seemed content grazing some fifty yards distant and had no serious interest in the visitors. He nudged his mount at a gallop toward the solitary horse. The animal did not object when he sidled in beside it and stretched from his saddle to grab its reins. The horse followed without resistance as Thad joined Kirsten near the former lodge location. They both dismounted when he got there.

Thad said, "One horse without a rider. I didn't notice what Dad was riding. As I told you, he came into the clinic to talk to me. I didn't even go outside with him when he left. I brushed him off, and it might have been the last time I'll see him alive."

"Don't start beating up on yourself. Most folks have those regrets after they've lost someone. I felt like that with my father. Besides, we don't know what's happened here yet."

"I don't like what I'm seeing right now."

"What do you mean?"

"Look up and in the direction of the canyon."

Kirsten turned her head toward the canyon. "Oh shit. Buzzards. Must be thirty of them at least."

The ominous black birds with outsized wingspans soared slowly and drifted low, some dropping intermittently from what seemed an almost synchronized ballet in the sky to disappear into the canyon's depths. Cinder sat whimpering on the canyon's edge.

"Go, Cinder." Thad commanded. The dog disappeared over the ledge. He turned to Kirsten. "She'll find whatever it is. Let's follow."

They scrambled down the trail they had negotiated just a few nights previous, neither speaking as they dodged through the brush. They took turns holding back low-hanging limbs and offering a shoulder for balance on the rutted, rocky path. Thad hoped they came up with a dead goat or deer at the end of their journey because he knew the buzzards had identified carrion, not live prey. They were nearly to the canyon floor when Cinder's barking broke the silence.

They followed her bark along the streambank until he caught sight of the dog on the trail ahead. As they neared, the dog abandoned her find and raced to meet them. He saw two bootless feet and a man's mutilated bare legs sprawled across the trail.

"Good girl," he said, patting the Dalmatian's head before he picked up the pace and headed toward the victim, praying silently that it was not his father and scolding himself for hoping it was someone else.

"It's George," Kirsten called from behind him. "You can see what's left of his face peering out under the gooseberry brambles. But the damn buzzards took his eyes and ripped skin and flesh from his cheeks."

When they reached the corpse, Thad winced at the sight. The buzzards had not waited for their meal to ripen. His killer had stripped the deputy down to his undershorts, and the scavengers had torn into those and removed the morsels underneath. Virtually no part of the man's body had been unviolated, but the bullet holes in his head and chest were evident.

"We'd better leave the body as it is for the sheriff to look at. Maybe we can go downstream and comb the slopes nearby to see if we can find anything else." Meaning Judge Myles Locke.

Kirsten said, "Why don't you take the area along the streambed. I'll go up the slope a bit and see if I can come up with anything that might help. We're not going to find anything, though."

"Why are you so sure?"

"Look up."

The buzzards were soaring in a tight circle above his head, waiting for the intruders to depart, so they could finish their meals. They did not appear to have a secondary quarry.

"I see what you mean."

"And nothing else has caught Cinder's attention."

"You're right. But let's look around anyway." He spoke to the Dalmatian. "Cinder. Stay." Then he turned to Kirsten, who was already climbing to higher ground. "Cinder will keep the buzzards away."

Thad and Kirsten searched the canyon for several hours before they returned to Cinder and George Stewart's body. Thad sat down on a nearby limestone boulder, and Kirsten leaned back against a gnarled oak. Thad noticed that his partner seemed unfazed by their strenuous morning, stunning in her exotic way as she stood there with her low-crowned hat pulled low on her forehead to ward off a sliver of sunlight that had slipped through the overhanging tree branches. Her short-cropped chestnut hair fell short of her shoulders.

"Why do you think the killer or killers took George's clothes?" Thad asked.

"If they're the same bastards who killed Granny—and it seems likely—for the same reason they took the goats. They had use for them."

"Seems too simple."

"Sometimes, Doc, you make things too damned complicated. You think too much. Dumb folks like me don't get our heads all bogged down with too many details."

"Yeah, I know how dumb you are," he said sarcastically. "You play the dumb game and skin every poor devil who does business with you. Since it's all so simple to you dumb folks, what's your theory about what happened to my dad?"

"Obvious. The killers took him with them. Just like the goats and the clothes, they had a use for him. The question is what they expect to use him for—and how long before they don't need him."

Of course, she made perfect sense. And he would have wasted time considering a dozen possibilities before he likely reached the same conclusion. Her mind was scary sometimes, quick as a copperhead's bite. But he was accustomed to her thinking and her seemingly rough ways, and he trusted her without question. Kirstin Cavelle always had his back, and when the chips were down, he had hers. She was his best friend and knew he was hers. So, why wouldn't she marry him?

"Well, then we'd better find Dad while they still have a use for him."

"Then you'd better not wait for Sam Mallery to find him."

"You don't like Sam much, do you?"

"He means well enough, I suppose. But he annoys me sometimes. Maybe it goes back to the time I spent in his accommodations before my trial. But let me ask you something. Are you really willing to wait on Sam Mallery to find your father?"

He deferred answering her question. "I think I have a poncho in my saddlebags. I'm going to bring it down here to cover up George. It seems indecent to leave him exposed like this." He stood up and started up the slope.

Kirsten followed him after telling Cinder to stay. "God knows I'm not going to wait here for Sam Mallery. He won't pay any attention to anything a woman has to say anyway."

When they reached the rim of the canyon, Thad saw the goat pen and walked over to it, his eyes scanning the interior.

"Enjoying the scenery?" Kirsten asked.

"This made me think of something Dad said when he stopped by the clinic. He told me he was going to look for something in the goat pen. He said he would tell me about it when I came in to his office to talk with him about Granny's business."

"Why would he need to talk with you about Granny's business?"

"Apparently I am named as an alternate executor and trustee of her will. I would serve if Dad wasn't able."

"You have no idea what he expected to find in the pen?"

"No. Something valuable, I assume."

"A pot of gold, perhaps?"

"I don't know. I suppose I need to come back with Dad and bring a good shovel and do some searching. But that's last on my priority list at the moment."

"I wonder if her killer was looking for the same thing?"

"Possible, I suppose."

"I don't think you should mention this to Mallery yet. With his big mouth this place will be swarming with fortune hunters an hour after he hits town."

"I hate to withhold information from the law, but I'm afraid you're right. And I don't see how this would help him find Dad."

"Speaking of the devil, there are riders coming this way—probably our good sheriff. There will just be a fuss if I stick around. Do you want me to ride into Manhattan and report to Vedette?"

"Do you have time?"

She gave him an annoyed look and ignored his question. She walked away and mounted her blue roan. As she rode away, he noted she was taking a route that would bypass the sheriff.

Chapter 14

MYLES LOCKE'S EYELIDS fluttered open to total blackness, and his first thought was that he had been blinded. He closed his eyes and sucked in a deep breath, taking a few moments to compose himself and collect recall of his last memories. He could tell that he was sprawled on his back on a cold, stone floor. He opened his eyes again, realizing now he was imprisoned within a windowless room or cave. He started to lift his head, but the lightning bolt that ripped through his skull forced him back. He lay there, trying desperately to orient himself. Where was he?

His panic eased when his eyes adjusted to the darkness, and he saw dim light hovering above him, evidently sifting through cracks between warped boards. He raised himself upon his elbows. When he lifted his head this time, the pain was less severe, but dizziness forced him back down. He drifted off to semi-consciousness for a time before he tried again. Finally, shucking the vertigo, he scooted back to a wall and inched his way into a sitting position. The effort sapped away what little strength he had, and he sighed heavily and leaned back to regroup his senses again. Some moments later, he gently brushed his fingertips tentatively over his right temple and was startled to find a lump the size of half an apple with a sticky groove splitting it. Then he realized his face was blood-caked, as was his shirt. His waistcoat and boots had also disappeared, but that was the least of his worries.

His eyes scanned the room, and he discovered a canteen within reach and a bucket in one corner, placed there for obvious purposes. He leaned to one side and stretched out his arm and grasped the canteen. He was relieved to find it was full, and a few seconds later, he pressed it to his lips and drank generously before reminding himself that he might need some of the water later.

More alert now, he studied his surroundings. The room appeared to be roughly square, possibly ten to a dozen feet in each direction. An old root cellar, perhaps? Or a storm shelter for refuge when the occasional Kansas tornado twisted and swept its devastating winds across the prairies and hills?

He guessed that the ceiling might be ten feet from the floor. He was a tall man but would not be able to touch it, let alone break through. The light slipping through the cracks seemed dim and filtered, and he figured that a house or structure of some type enclosed the space above. Regardless, Myles decided he was confined in a deep pit. No steps or ladder. But there had to be an entryway, or how had he ended up here?

Slowly, Myles twisted his lean frame and got on his hands and knees, and then, bracing against the solid limestone wall, he raised himself upright, before resting again to fight off the dizziness. Now he could view his ceiling, which he concluded was someone else's floor. And near one wall, he could make out the outline of a trapdoor, perhaps a yard square, in the ceiling. It was likely locked in some fashion, although it did not matter if he had no ladder to facilitate his escape.

Exhausted from his efforts, Myles let himself down on the floor again, his back pressed against the wall beneath the trapdoor. It had been an ambitious project, he thought, for someone to take pick, sledge, and shovel to excavate this cavern, although limestone was generally brittle and would break off in chunks and small pieces with less effort than most stone. But for what purpose? Then he spied something on the floor in one corner of his prison. It was too dark to identify so he crawled across the floor to investigate. But he stopped short when he comprehended what he had discovered. A cluster of bones tangled with fragments of cloth, human remains with a naked skull positioned face-upward in the middle of the nest. Then, beside it, he saw another skull amid scattered bones. He backed away and positioned himself nearby against the wall again.

Was this his fate? To starve in this death pit and eventually make another contribution to this collection of bones? He did not fear death. His religious beliefs were vague and unsettled. There was either an afterlife or there was not. His life was much too busy for him to dwell on the issue. It was the process of dying that sometimes worried him. He aspired to die bravely and stoically, but he was not confident he had such courage, and, of course, would not know until the test came. And perhaps it was upon him now.

But if he was to simply wait in this cold hole for death to visit, why had his captors provided water? They must have some temporary use for him, some reason to keep him alive for the moment.

"What's your name, mister?"

He started when he heard the voice from above. It was muffled, but it was clearly a child's, probably a little girl. It did not matter. He had human contact, and he intended to hang on to it. "My name is Myles. What is your name?"

"My name is Regina. But Mama always called me Gina."

"What should I call you?"

"Gina would be nice."

"How old are you, Gina?"

"I think I am seven. But I'm not sure. Mama used to tell me when she was here."

"Where is your mother?"

"She is down there with you, I think. Cyrus said she died in hell."

My God. Was the girl's mother one of his skeletal companions? "Am I in hell? Is that what this place is called?"

"Yes. This is where Cyrus puts people who have been bad. Sometimes just for a day. Some stay for a long time. Mama and Nathaniel stayed forever. Do you see Mama there?"

"Uh, no, I don't, Gina."

"Agatha said you can't see people when they are dead. They are invisible. And I always watched the door to hell, and I never saw Mama come out. I think she is there. You just can't see her."

"Who are Cyrus and Agatha?"

"Cyrus tells everybody what to do. They call him Lord Cyrus. Agatha is our witch and rules the wives."

He could not fathom what the girl was talking about. It seemed she was lost in a fairy tale. But he believed he was in hell. And he suspected he was sharing it with the remains of the little girl's mother and Nathaniel. He hesitated to ask her the question, but he decided to forge ahead. "Where is your father?"

"I'm not sure. Cyrus used to be my father. Then he said Nathaniel was my father. That was when the tribe beat my mother and Nathaniel, and Cyrus sent them to hell. I might not have a father. Cyrus told me I was Satan's spawn. I don't know what that is, but I think Satan's the devil, isn't he?"

The girl was obviously confused, but he noticed she spoke well, using the English language quite properly for one so young. "Where do you go to school?"

"School is against the rules here. But I know my numbers, and I can read. But not anymore since my books were burned. Mama taught me these things until Lord Cyrus found out and she got a whipping on her bare back and butt in front of the tribe. She told me after that not to tell anyone, but she and Nathaniel were going to take me away soon. After that they were sent to hell."

"How did you know I was here?"

"I saw Timothy and Reuben bring you to Peace Commune yesterday afternoon. They led your horse here. You were thrown over its back. I thought you were dead, and I saw them take you to hell."

"And you came to see?"

"I sneak in here every morning. I feel Mama near when I am in the barn and near hell. I heard you moving."

"So this is in a barn?"

"A big barn. Some horses are kept here. Lots of hay. Hell is covered with hay if outsiders come. I must go now. I hear somebody outside. I will come back tomorrow."

"Thank you, Gina. I will look forward to that."

Soon after the girl departed, he heard scuffling on the ground above. Then the trapdoor rattled, and someone pulled it open and knelt to peer in the pit. Myles recognized the face as that of the large, bearded man who had confronted him in the canyon and presumably struck him.

"Hey, law wrangler, you awake down there?" the man called.

Myles replied, "Yes, I am conscious."

"Here." The man dropped something through the opening and it struck the floor of the pit. "Make that and your water do till tomorrow night. I ain't bringing no more."

Myles crawled nearer to the opening and looked up, trying to evaluate the structure of the door, but the ugly man's head and torso blocked his view. He felt the object that had been pitched into his dungeon and concluded it was a partial loaf of crusty bread.

"You didn't ask about tomorrow night," came the gravelly voice from above.

"I didn't know a response was required. What happens tomorrow night?"

"You go before the tribal council and they decide what to do with you. I promise they ain't going to turn you loose. It'll be damn fun to see what they come up with." He dropped the door, leaving Myles to ponder his fate.

Chapter 15

WHEN KIRSTEN ARRIVED at the Myles Locke home, she noticed Cameron Locke's Appaloosa stallion tied to one of the hitching posts in front of the white, two-story house. Of course, he would have been in the Locke offices by the time Ned returned to town, and Vedette would have sent word about Cam's missing father. She liked Cam, but he was something of a dandy and tended to shove others aside quickly to take charge of any crisis, some of this trait likely stemming from his experience as a former Confederate cavalry officer. Kirsten was better acquainted with his wife, Pilar, the only child of an Old South Texas Spanish family, who was one of the investors in Medicine Wheel Properties.

Vedette came to the front door in response to Kirsten's soft knocking. When she opened the door, she appeared surprised to see Kirsten and looked at her questioningly.

Kirsten said, "I told Thad I would bring you a report."

Vedette waved her in, and Kirsten entered the parlor where Cam, dressed in expensive boots and charcoal-colored suit, sat with a worried-looking Ned. The rangy lawyer stood when he saw Kirsten, his greenish-brown eyes meeting hers.

"Kirsten, do you have news about Dad?"

"I guess you would call it an update. We still don't know where he is." She went on to relate what she knew of Deputy Stewart's death. "The sheriff was arriving as I left. Thad was going to lead him to the body and see if he can do anything to help. There was no sign of Myles or his horse any place."

Cam said, "That makes no sense if he went to Granny's with Stewart. If he somehow escaped an ambush, he would have hightailed it for Medicine Wheel."

"Unless he was forced to hide out some place—or was captured."

"But why would anyone abduct my father? Makes no sense."

Vedette interrupted. "At least there is hope he's alive."

"Yes," Cam said. "And now we've got to find him. And I am sure as hell not going to wait on Sam Mallery to do it.

I'm riding back out to the Circle L. I'll get my son, Wrangler, and a few of the hands, and we'll go out to Granny Gray Owl's place and start our own search."

Kirsten said, "If I start back to Medicine Wheel, I should meet up with Thad on the road, if he's not still with the sheriff. We can call out the fire volunteers to get more searchers, but I'm afraid it will be getting too close to sundown to look for very long. If we don't have any luck, I'm sure most of the boys would be ready to go again at sunrise."

"I would appreciate that. I'll likely stay the night just to be out there on the chance I'd hear something. I'm sure Sam won't have any help rounded up before tomorrow morning."

Vedette said, "It's not my decision, Cam, but do you think your brothers and sister should be notified?"

"Nothing they can do, but I suppose they're entitled to know. Can't tell them much by telegraph but can at least prepare them in case we've got bad news later. Ian and Hannah are easy enough to find, but God knows where Franklin is. He rides that Methodist circuit all over Nebraska, sometimes north into South Dakota. I'll check with Reva. She may know something and would send the messages if I work with her on the wording."

Cam rushed out the door without another word. Kirsten turned to Vedette. "I can't tell you not to worry, but I think Myles is alive. But if you're a praying woman, you might take time to put in a good word up there." She stepped toward Vedette and gave her a quick hug.

She looked over at Ned who sat silently and glumly on the settee. "Ned, you've done good work today. It's important that you be with your grandma now."

"Yes, ma'am."

Kirsten started for the door when Vedette said, "I am a praying woman, and I've been doing a lot of it these past hours. But I don't believe the Almighty just waves a magic wand to solve these things. I think He's put this mission on the shoulders of you and Thad."

Church-going had not been a habit of Kirsten's since her mother died on the family's Missouri ranch and left her to grow up with six older brothers and a doting father, who mostly knew how to raise sons. But Vedette's words somehow struck a chord in her soul and weighed heavily upon her.

Chapter 16

THAD AND KIRSTEN reined in their mounts near the ruins of Granny's former lodge once again. They had recruited Red Holiday and six other volunteers for the search, deciding that the remaining half dozen volunteers in the Medicine Wheel vicinity should remain available for a possible fire call. Thad instructed a disappointed Cinder to stay at the fire hall this outing. He suspected the dog was looking for an opportunity to escape from Socks for a spell. Cinder obviously felt responsible for the clinging kid and had genuine affection for the foundling but, like many new mothers, welcomed an occasional reprieve.

Thad looked around but saw no sign of the sheriff. He guessed Sam Mallery had returned to Manhattan with his deputy and George Stewart's body. Presumably he would return tomorrow with some searchers. The volunteers

Ron Schwab

had borrowed a buckboard from Red and loaded food supplies for a several-day stay. Each had bedrolls, and a fair number of wedge-shaped, two-person pup tents had been confiscated from the fire hall supply room.

They decided to set up camp near the building site before starting the search. The well assured a fresh, ample water supply, the scene of the murders seemed the logical starting place. Thad hoped Cam would arrive soon so they could coordinate their efforts. He knew, also, that his older brother had Indian-like tracking abilities that might serve the search well. As the volunteers pulled the tents and gear from the wagon, Kirsten slipped in beside Thad, and in a near whisper, asked, "Are we sharing a tent?"

"I'll help set up a tent for you, but we're not going to share one."

"That's what I thought. You can be such a prude sometimes. Everybody knows we sleep together."

"Everybody knows we're not married, and they only suspect we sleep together. I don't think we should furnish public confirmation."

She smiled mischievously at him, and he realized she had been deviling him again. He admitted he tended to be too serious and strait-laced sometimes. The enigmatic Kirsten had a knack for lightening such moments. Of course, she would have shared his tent willingly. She did not care what anyone thought. But for Thad marriage would make their lives much less complicated. Or more so.

As the volunteers finished setting up camp, Cam Locke rode in with his sixteen-year-old son, Wrangler, and two other riders. Trailing behind was a chuckwagon, which explained Cam's delay. Cookie Colyer, a scraggly-bearded, sharp-tongued old timer would be driving, and there would be only one cook in the outdoor kitchen. And the searchers would be well-fed.

Cam and Wrangler dismounted and walked toward Thad and Kirsten. Thad noted that Wrangler, whose given name was Myles, had recently edged past his father's six-feet-two inches height. Tall and rangy, they both walked alike with a bit of a swagger, but the resemblance ended there. Cam, in his mid-forties, had white-flecked sandy-hair and piercing steel-gray eyes and could not resist flamboyance with his black Stetson and matching boots and vest, all nicely cleaned and polished. Wrangler, on the other hand, had his Spanish mother's dark coloring and soft coffee-brown eyes and was clothed like a saddle tramp. And though Cam would not admit it, the young man's reputation as a horseman already exceeded his father's. Thad thought the odds of Wrangler being sucked into his namesake's profession were slim. The young man's destiny was ranching, and it might not be in the Flint Hills. He was committed to spend next summer as a vaquero on his grandfather's South Texas ranch.

Cam doffed his Stetson and then extended his hand to Thad, who tried not to wince when the vice clamped down. "Cookie said it would be sundown before he would have supper ready. What can we do before then?"

"Nobody's ever done a complete search of the canyon below or even of the tallgrass surrounding the building site. I'd like to show you where George's body was found. I thought at first light you might want to see if you can pick up sign from there."

"Makes sense. Who commands your volunteers?"

"Red Holiday. He's the volunteer chief. I don't think he considers himself a commander."

"The freighter? I know him." He turned away and surveyed the gathering and spotted Red and walked away.

Wrangler grinned. "Pop's going to tell Red what to do. That's what he does—is tell people what to do. I suppose you know that."

"Well sometimes somebody's got to be in charge. Does he tell you what to do?"

"Oh, yeah. Sometimes, I listen. Other times I'm sort of hard of hearing. He doesn't mean anything by it. Mom says he never left the army. Of course, he doesn't even try to tell mom what to do."

Chapter 17

THE SEARCHERS HAD risen and finished eating before sunrise, and Cam directed his Circle L crew to comb the canyon rim and adjacent grasslands for at least a mile to the northeast. He had instructed the fire brigade volunteers to split up and walk each side of the canyon walls to search for evidence that Myles Locke had been there or to recover his body should it be hidden in the trees or undergrowth. Wrangler was to lead the horses along the northerly rim while Cam, Thad, and Kirsten worked the canyon floor along the stream.

The previous night Thad and Kirsten had shown Cam the spot on the trail where Deputy Stewart's body had been discovered. Thad's elder brother was impatient to return in good light to inspect the area and to trek up the narrow canyon to the northeast, convinced that that no other direction made any sense considering the location of the body from the lodge ruins. Also, the goats and mule appeared to have been herded off in that direction.

As they hiked up the canyon, Cam ranged both sides of the stream like a bird-dog. Abruptly, he stopped and knelt. "Hoofprints in the mud here along the bank. Shoe prints, too. Not boots. Seems likely somebody planned on walking in to Granny's place. One horse. They're obviously leading the critter. Could be the Judge's mount. Question is whether he was on it, or the killers just stole a horse."

They walked a bit more than a half-mile along the stream, and it appeared to Thad there was no attempt by the pursued to cover their tracks. Over-confident or just stupid?

Wrangler called from the canyon rim, "Pop. I think you need to come up and take a look. Signs that they came out up here."

Kirsten spotted a winding deer trail that threaded through the brush and led to the top, and the trio scrambled up the steep slope and soon stepped onto the dry grassy carpet covering the canyon's fringe. Wrangler waited there with the mounts he had been leading.

Wrangler pointed to an area of stomped-down grass decorated with several mounds of horse dung. "Looks like somebody kept some horses here for a spell and then rode off that way." He pointed northeasterly toward a towering tree that was the sole landmark in the middle of a rolling sea of hills and grass.

"Peace Commune." Kirsten said softly. "I should have thought of that."

"What are you talking about?" Cam asked.

"They live on the old Graham quarter section about two miles beyond that big tree. I think Frank Graham sold the place to some of the folks who live there. The whole quarter is fenced in with barbed wire. There is one gate, and there is generally somebody posted there. I've ridden around the outside some, scouting it out for possible purchase someday."

"Is there anything you haven't scouted out for purchase?" Cam asked.

"I just keep my eyes out for possibilities. Anyway, it looks pitiful the last I saw it. They planted some of the ground to corn, and it looks near death. We all know the uplands here aren't fit to grow row crops. The weeds have taken over, and the plants have dried up. Looks like they just planted it and left it on its own, I'll bet they don't yield a bushel out of the forty some acres taken up by the crop. The grass isn't so bad some places. Some of it has been cut for hay it appears, and when I was up there a few months back, I couldn't see more than a half dozen cows grazing out there. They were scroungy-looking critters, but there was plenty of grass to eat."

"How many people live at the farm?" Thad asked. "I've heard of the community but never met anybody from there that I'm aware of. Quincy Belmont's had some dealings with a few men from the place and seems to know a little about it. He said it's one of those settlements where the property is held in common. Everybody contributes what they can, and they all share what's produced equally."

Kirsten replied, "That explains the sick condition of the corn acres. They're running a little short on the contribution side, I'd guess. And it's easy enough to split nothing. But to answer your question. It appears there are a good number of folks on the place but couldn't guess how many. I looked the residential compound over from a knoll-top with my telescope, and there was lots of activity there. Women and kids scurrying about. Only a few men in sight, and they weren't scurrying. Besides the old two-story farm house, I'd guess there were nearly a dozen temporary structures with canvas stretched over wood frames. Housing, I suppose, but I'd sure hate to be living in those things when winter comes."

"Outbuildings?" Cam asked.

"Big barn. In fair shape yet. Run-down stable and a chicken house and a few storage-sheds. And at least two outhouses. It appeared they were trying to stack a wall of rock to enclose the compound, but they hadn't got far. Likely short of volunteers. And they may claim the land's owned in common, but the county clerk's records show the quarter is titled in the name of one Cyrus Crabbe."

Cam said, "I think we'd better ride over and visit this Peace Commune."

Thad said, "It sounds like a place that could make use of goats and a mule and anything else edible."

"Wrangler," Cam directed, "get word to the boys that we're riding off for a few hours. Then turn around and catch up with us. We'll be moving slow and cautious."

Without a word the boy effortlessly swung his horse around and shortly disappeared into the hills.

Chapter 18

B Y THE TIME Wrangler returned the riders could see a plume of smoke rising from the earth not too far distant, the source hidden behind the hills of tallgrass.

Kirsten said, "Follow me. I know where the best over-look is." She veered away and eased her mount toward one of the larger flattop hills that were plentiful in the Kansas Flint Hills. When they reached the top of the steep incline, the riders dismounted, and Kirsten plucked a mariner's telescope from her saddlebags.

She handed the telescope to Cam. "Buildings and gate are on this side of the quarter section. You can see the layout quite well from here."

Cam silently studied the compound site for some minutes before he spoke. "There's a guard at the gate. I wonder what would happen if I rode down there to inquire about the Judge."

"Not alone," Thad said. "I'll go with you."

Cam shrugged and replied, "Let's all go make the visit. Maybe a show of force will shake something up."

They mounted their horses, and Cam moved out in front as they rode down the gentle slope toward the gate. The guard caught sight of them when they were less than fifty yards distant and immediately raised his rifle and fired three shots into the air. Thad gathered this was a signal to his comrades rather than a warning to the approaching strangers. As they neared, the scrawny, rat-faced man leveled his rifle waist high in their direction. He looked over his shoulder to see if help was coming, and when he saw no one, he began to fidget nervously. Thad noted that he wore tattered bib overalls and a ragged straw hat and ankle-high work shoes. More sodbuster than cowboy, he figured. The guard did not appear all that comfortable with a rifle in his hands.

The man cleared his throat and spoke with a high-pitched, shaky voice. "That's far enough, folks. This here is private property."

They pulled up about ten feet from the splintered gate, and the guard remained on the opposite side. Cam said, "We mean no harm. We're looking for my father,

Judge Myles Locke. He's missing and was last seen out this way."

Panic flashed in the man's eyes, and he cast a glance over his shoulder again. This time he was rewarded with the sight of three riders moving their horses at a gallop down the rutted trail from the direction of the compound. The guard turned back to Cam, noticeably relieved. "Lord Cyrus is coming. You can ask him about your father. I got no more to say."

As the riders reached the gate, the first thing Thad's practiced eye noticed was the condition of the horses. They were seriously malnourished, ribs sharply outlined against their hides, shoulder and hip bones protruding. The horses' eyes were glazed and matted with pus and wet streaks in the hair below indicated the flowing of tears from infected eyes. He looked at Kirsten and saw that her attention was fixed on the horses as well, her lips pressed together tightly and her eyes spitting fire.

A slender, almost effeminate-looking man with black hair curling out from beneath a planter's hat and neatly-trimmed moustache and goatee, sidled his horse up next to the gate. He spoke first to the guard. "What seems to be the trouble here, Wallace?"

"These folks is looking for some judge feller, Lord."

Lord? The man looked like the Devil more than God. And royal titles were generally ignored in America. But he was certainly elegantly dressed, attired in white shirt and string tie and shiny black fox-hunting boots that covered the calves of his legs.

The man turned his head toward the visitors, and his dark eyes scanned each of them appraisingly, pausing a moment at Kirsten and doffing his hat and offering a small smile, before directing his words to Cam. "And your name?"

"Cameron Locke. And yours?"

"I am Cyrus Crabbe. I am the governor of Peace Commune."

"Well, Crabbe, we're looking for my father, Judge Myles Locke." Cam was clearly intentionally ignoring the man's title.

"A judge, no less."

"Former judge. Have you or any of your people seen my father? He's a bit past seventy, white hair, six-feet tall. Looks like an older version of my brother, Doctor Thad Locke, here." Cam nodded to Thad, who was saddled to his right.

The man hesitated, and his eyes narrowed before he replied. "We haven't seen your father. We haven't had any visitors here all summer, and none of our people have been absent from the commune for at least two weeks."

Thad thought the man was a bit too precise with his response. He noticed the other men eyeing each other nervously.

Cam said, "Do you mind if we come in and talk to some of your people? We won't take long."

"I do mind. I told you none of our people have seen your father."

"We would appreciate your cooperation. Otherwise, we will force a search of your property. It happens Granny Gray Owl, a neighbor of yours, was murdered and her place burned out a few days back, and we're investigating that, too."

"Never heard of the woman."

"She had a place southwest of here—about four miles as the crow flies."

"I don't know the place."

"We expect to search your commune."

"I have fifteen men here and twice that many women and children. Everybody big enough to hold a rifle can and will use it. And I don't see a badge on your shirt, Locke. Now get the hell out of here."

Crabbe wheeled his horse away and headed the mount at a lope back toward the compound. His companions remained with the guard, one a huge scraggly-bearded man, and the other a young, fuzzy-cheeked man who was rail-thin and obviously uncomfortable astride a horse. The big man glared menacingly at the visitors and looked like he was spoiling for a fight. Cam scowled back, as if daring him to make a move.

Thad said calmly, "Cam, we need to talk about this. Let's get out of here." He turned his horse back toward the hills above the commune property, and Kirsten fell in beside him, leaving Cam alone in his stare-down. Finally, he said, "You've done something with my father. If you've got him here and turn him over peaceably, you'll live. If he's dead, so are you." He rode away and joined the others.

By the time they reined in behind an outcropping of rocks, Cam had cooled and turned strategist again. "These people had something to do with Granny's murder and they're either holding the Judge for some purpose or have already killed him. If he's alive, I don't think they will harm him—not yet, anyway. They're figuring he might be a ticket out."

"We've got to go in," Thad said, "but we need the sheriff and a good number of fighting men. I wonder if we could get help from Fort Riley?"

"We don't have time to go through the Army bureaucrats. This is a civilian matter, and they would need orders from President Cleveland himself to help us. And we need to strike tomorrow morning before they have time to think too much about this or pull out."

"If they have as many people there as they claim, they aren't going to be clearing out too fast."

"I'm going to talk to Sheriff Mallery and push him to get a search warrant from the county judge. Mallery wouldn't usually worry about a warrant, but he will be spooked about this and looking for excuses to back off. We'll use Granny's place as a headquarters and have everybody rendezvous there. Thad, can you round up some more men that are willing to use a gun, if necessary?"

"I'm sure the volunteers from the fire brigade that are out here will stick around. I can ride in to Medicine Wheel and round up more help. Quincy Belmont's an ex-buffalo soldier. I'm sure he would sign on. He has a few former soldiers working for him, too."

"We need to have somebody keep an eye on the commune," Cam said. "We've got to know if anybody goes in or out and keep track of what's happening in the compound as much as we can. Wrangler, can you do that? Maybe Kirsten can loan you the telescope."

"I'll stay with him," Kirsten said. "Just in case another gun is needed."

"You sure?"

"I wouldn't have said so otherwise."

"We're about high noon. I'll send somebody over to relieve you before nightfall."

Kirsten replied, "We'll take care of it until somebody shows up."

Chapter 19

KIRSTEN AND WRANGLER staked their horses behind the limestone outcropping and crept through the dips between the hills until they found the little flattop butte that previously served as their spy nest. This time they took more care to avoid being sighted by their quarry and crawled behind the cover of a cluster of small boulders. Kirsten figured a telescope aimed in their direction from the compound would still pick up their presence, but that was a risk she would have to take.

Fortunately, they had each stashed a few biscuits from morning's breakfast in their saddlebags, and Wrangler had an ample supply of beef jerky he shared with Kirsten. They ate silently at their perch on the butte, checking the commune site frequently to monitor activity there. Kirsten noticed Wrangler trying to study her surreptitiously as they ate, and she flattered herself to think the boy might be a bit taken with her—physically at least. She supposed teenage boys were not all that discerning in their tastes, however. He likely was just mentally un-clothing her.

The sun bathed them with warm rays, luring them both to drowsiness, so they decided to keep watch in one-hour shifts. Kirsten was stretched out on the ground, napping after taking first shift when Wrangler shook her shoulder and startled her awake.

"Kirsten, come look at this. A woman's running away from the compound toward the fence."

Wrangler handed her the telescope, and she scooted to a position behind the boulders and raised the instru-ment to her eye, adjusting it until she brought the com-pound clearly into view. "I'm not seeing her," she said.

"More to the north. She's running west."

Kirsten angled the telescope northward, and then she picked up the movement of a black-haired woman running across the grass stubble. She stumbled and fell several times but recovered and kept on her course, al-though she appeared unsteady on her legs. As the wom-an drew nearer and approached the four-strand barbed wire fence, Kirsten could see her long dress was tattered and she was barefoot. She eased the telescope back toward the compound and saw now that a man with pistol in hand was giving chase.

The woman reached the fence and dropped to the ground to squeeze under the bottom wire just as the pistol cracked. When a barb snagged the woman's dress and seemed to have thwarted the escape, Kirsten passed the telescope to Wrangler and scrambled up and raced for her horse. "Stay here," she instructed the boy.

She leaped into the saddle and reined her gelding in the direction of the chase. As she emerged from the hills, she saw that the woman had torn herself free from the barb, leaving much of the skirt of her dress on the fence wire. She was moving faster now with just her bloomers covering her thighs and unencumbered by the skirt. She was obviously headed for a small canyon with the tops of oak and ash trees peering over the top. Good thinking. The man had encountered a delay at the fence as well. A stocky man, he had tried to slip between the middle wires and was hung up there for the moment. It appeared a barb had caught him at the crotch of his trousers. She hoped he left one of his testicles on the wire. She reined her mount northwest between the knolls, intent on intercepting the woman at the canyon rim.

When she broke onto the flatter prairie and tallgrass that lay west of the commune property, she saw that the pursuer had escaped his trap and was gaining ground on his prey, probably only fifty or sixty feet behind. He stopped and fired again, but the woman remained on her feet. Kirsten urged her blue roan forward, pushing the animal toward the man, who was still fifty yards distant, as she closed in from the south. She slipped her Colt from its holster and fired several shots in the air to claim his attention. The ruse worked. He stopped and turned toward her. He fired his gun, but the distance was too great, and she suspected he was not a marksman in any case. As she drew within firing range, she reined in her horse and quickly dismounted, disappearing in some four-foot high tallgrass.

She knew the man was focused on her, and the escapee should have slipped into the protection of the canyon trees by now. Keeping her head down, she crept in the direction of the gunman.

"Come on out, you cowardly bastard," came a shaky voice. "Be a man."

She smiled at his misidentification but remained silent. He was afraid, and she planned to feed his fear. She fired her Colt into the air again and quickly crawled to another spot. Her adversary fired his gun again, but he apparently had no idea where she was at. Then she heard swishing of the grass from his position. He was running toward the compound. She stood and yelled, "Stop."

The man halted and swung around. His eyes widened in disbelief when he saw her. "A woman. I don't believe this."

Her gender evidently called up his bravado again. "You stupid bitch. Today you die."

He barely raised his pistol before Kirsten's first bullet tore into his chest. Before he tumbled over, her next bullet bored a third eye in his head. Then she retrieved her blue roan, which had backed off a short distance but remained within summoning range. She led the horse to the canyon's edge and saw that it was no more than forty feet in depth, although sloping steeply, typical of the countless small canyons and arroyos that crisscrossed the Flint Hills. Her eyes scanned the trees and undergrowth, but she saw no sign of the woman.

"Ma'am, you are safe now," she called. "The man who was chasing you is dead. I am here to help you."

Silence.

"Can you hear me? Please come out. I promise you will not be harmed."

The brush rustled some twenty feet down the slope, and the woman slipped from behind a wide, ancient oak. But she wasn't a woman. She was a girl a few years short of full-fledged womanhood. And the dirt smudges and bruises on her face could not hide her dark beauty.

She walked slowly up the slope, pushing back the brambles and branches that bit at her flesh. When she reached the top, Kirsten saw that the girl was trembling, and she stepped forward and welcomed the girl into her arms and held her as she broke into uncontrolled sobbing. The girl was nearly five and a half feet tall, but she would not weigh one hundred pounds, and her frail frame suggested near starvation.

"What is your name, dear?" Kirsten asked, still holding her close.

"Martha," she said, "but my folks always called me Marty. I like that."

"Marty, we need to get out of here. Somebody else may be coming to see what happened. Can you ride behind me on my horse? We don't have far to go."

"Yes, I think so."

A few minutes later, Kirstin and Marty rode back into the surrounding hills, Marty's arms clasped tightly about Kirsten's back.

Wrangler had evidently followed the action from his position on the butte because he spoke to Kirsten excitedly as she joined him at the top. "Holy Moses, Kirsten. I didn't know you were a gunfighter. I've never seen anything like that."

Kirsten shrugged off the compliment. "Marty, this is Myles Locke. Folks call him Wrangler."

Wrangler's eyes fastened on Marty's, and Kirsten knew the new arrival had already crowded the older woman out of his heart. "Hi, Marty. Welcome. I was worried about you for a spell. That varmint chasing after you meant business."

"I decided I was going to get out of that place or die trying. It's a death trap anyway."

"What do you mean?" Kirsten asked. "And Wrangler, please keep looking to see if anybody is riding out to check on the gunfire."

"The council has decided to set fire to all the buildings and tent homes in the morning with all the commune members except the council and four or five loyal men shut up in the big house. After some folks came to the gate, they knew trouble was on the way. They figure they can escape while the fire is going. The authorities won't know if everybody died or not, and there won't be any witnesses alive to cause trouble."

"How do you know this?" Kirsten asked.

"Lady Agatha ordered me to the house today to help her pack some things—she didn't say why. The coun-

Ron Schwab

cil meets in one of the rooms there. While I was on my way to her room, I noticed a meeting was in session. I stopped outside the door and listened. I knew something big was going on. When I heard what they were saying, I just took off out the front door. Almost knocked Chester over. He was the guard there and should have been watching the council door. That's why he was after me."

"My God. What kind of people are these?"

"Evil. Lord Crabbe and his wife, Agatha, decide everything. My mother joined the commune before we came to Kansas more than five years ago. It sounded so good because everyone was to work in peace and harmony for the good of the commune, and then all the food and goods would be divided equally. But it didn't turn out that way. Lord Crabbe and Agatha and the council got what they wanted first and, if there was anything left, the others divided that. My mother protested three years back and said we were leaving. She disappeared the next day. I know somebody killed her."

"I must know one more thing and then we'll talk about this later. We are looking for an elderly man—Wrangler's grandfather. We suspect he is in the commune compound some place. Do you know anything about this?"

"That must be the man they brought back yesterday. He was tossed over a horse."

"Was he alive?"

"Yes. Gina told me they put him in hell, and she talked to him."

"Hell? What do you mean? And who is Gina?"

"Hell is a pit inside the barn where they lock up people who have misbehaved or broken rules of the commune. Most get out after their punishment, but I think Gina's mother and her lover died there almost two years ago. Gina's a little girl. She says her mother is still in hell, and she goes there because she can feel her presence. That's how she met the old man. I wish I could have brought Gina with me, but I never would have made it through the fence with her, and we would both be dead. I hoped I would find help. I guess I did."

Wrangler said, "Kirsten, there's no sign of anybody coming out the gate. Strange because they had to hear the shots."

"Not so strange," Marty said. "They're cowards. They might think all the gunshots came from Chester's gun and that he'll be coming back to tell them he killed me or is still chasing me. But if they thought somebody was shooting at Chester, they'd leave him on his own."

Kirsten thought about what she had been told. Cam and Thad needed to know about the possibility of a fire. If they worked through the night, they could have the volunteer brigade and fire-fighting equipment there before sunrise. It would be a long trip, though, following wagon roads and trails.

"You want me to ride, don't you, Kirsten?" Wrangler asked.

"Yes, Wrangler. Leave word at Granny's if your dad's not there. Then head for Medicine Wheel and tell your Uncle Thad to get the volunteer brigade and all the equipment as near to Peace Commune as they can without being discovered by the occupants."

Chapter 20

YLES HEARD MOVEMENT near the trapdoor. He tensed, hoping it was his little friend, Gina, but worried that he was about to receive another visit from his captors. He required time to think about his dilemma and work out a solution, although he knew he was deluding himself that his imprisonment was anything like a legal problem he could solve by just putting his mind to it. He had not an iota of control here.

"Hey, mister," came the familiar voice. "Are you still in hell?"

He found himself surrendering a small smile despite his circumstances. "Yes, Gina, I'm still here. I'm happy you came to visit me."

"I'm afraid, mister. Something is happening. The Lord is mad and upset."

"What is he mad about?"

"Some men came to the gate looking for somebody. One of the common wives said she heard there was a lady with them. I think they were looking for you."

A ray of hope slipped through the crack in the trapdoor with her words. "Did she say anything else?"

"She said two of the men rode white horses with either black or brown splotches on them. They wanted to come in and look for you, and when the Lord told them to go away, their leader said they would be back."

Horses with splotches. Probably Appaloosa. That would have be Cam and likely Thad—possibly young Myles, too. If there was a woman with them, he would bet on Kirsten Cavelle. They had evidently figured out he was being held at this place, but could they find him before these crazy people killed him? "Thank you, Gina, that's very helpful. And thank you for being my friend. A couple of the men who came to the gate were probably my sons."

"Will they take you away from here?"

"I hope so."

"If they take you, can I go with you?"

How selfish of him. He had not even considered the fate of this little girl. "Yes, if that's what you want. I will not leave without you." How else could he put it when his own future was far from certain?

"Something else happened."

"What's that?"

"Marty ran away."

"Who is Marty?"

"One of the older girls. She's always in trouble. She was put in hell once. I talked to her many times then. She has been horsewhipped at the stake at least two times. She's nice. She's my friend, and I told her about you. She does not want to be here, and I don't either. I am mad at her because she ran away without me. But I love her, too. Can that be?"

"Oh yes, loving somebody does not keep you from being angry at that person sometimes."

"I am afraid they killed her."

"Why do you think that?"

"Chester went after her, and we heard gunshots. But he hasn't come back yet. One of the wives thinks he is burying her some place and trying to hide her so those men don't find her. Anyway, something is happening. Everybody is all excited, and some are scared. Like me."

"What time is it now? Do you know?"

"I do not know how to tell time with a clock. And the house clock is broken anyway. But the sun is not high in the sky now, but I think it is a long way from night."

"Where was the sun when the visitors came to the gate?"

"The highest of all. Noontime."

If Cam and Thad left to get reinforcements, they would not be returning anytime soon. "You said people are excited and scared. Why?"

"They think the men will come back with others. The Lord says they will try to kill the men and take the women for themselves. I don't know what they will do with the kids. The council is going to meet soon. Everybody is to come to the big house tonight. Some think we are going to leave this place and go somewhere else."

"If these men come, go to the lady or one of the men on a spotted horse, if you can do so safely. They will protect you. Tell them where I am at."

"Hey, you little shit. What the hell do you think you're doing? No talking to prisoners. You know that." It was a booming voice, and Myles thought he recognized it as Reuben's.

The girl screamed, and he could hear a scuffle before all went silent. The clasp on the trapdoor rattled and then it swung open wide, admitting some light to his dark dungeon. His eyes squinted in response, even though there was no more than a dusky beam dropping through the opening.

"Where's Gina? What did you do with her?"

Reuben held the limp body of a tiny girl with dirty, tangled blonde hair over the opening. "Catch," he yelled before releasing his grip and dropping the girl through the opening. Reflexively, Myles' arms shot out to break her fall, and he caught her before tumbling to the floor with the dead weight of the child pinning him for a moment. Meanwhile, Reuben roared with laughter.

Myles scooted out from under the girl, and, sitting beside her, lifted her head and shoulders into his lap cradling her as best he could. His fingers traced a bloody lump on her forehead, a smaller version of his own wound. She was breathing and moving her head from side to side so he thought she was just stunned. He heard something strike the rock floor and looked up and saw that Reuben had lowered a ladder into the pit.

"Get up here," the big man ordered.

"The girl," Myles stammered. "I need to stay with her."

"Like hell you do. She just got a little tap from my pistol butt. And if you don't come out, she's going to get a bullet from the other end. You've got a meeting with the council."

Chapter 21

THE SUN'S RAYS were like a warm caress to Myles's back after being shut in his cool, damp underground prison for several days, and he found himself energized and hopeful. He knew that the surge could be short-lived, however, and he was eager to return to Gina. She had seemed more stunned than unconscious when he placed her near the wall, as far from the skeletal remains as he could. He had admonished her to lie still and not to move about the chamber, promising he would return soon but knowing that he might not.

The man called Reuben clutched Myles's forearm in an iron grip and half-drug him across the compound's grounds toward a two-story, weathered frame house. There was a stench in the air, and he soon realized it was coming from piles of rotting garbage—and perhaps worse—scattered with seeming randomness about the area. These were people who appeared to have no pride in the premises they occupied or were too lazy to set up a proper disposal site to deal with sanitation issues. He saw only a few clusters of men, some seriously emaciated and standing listlessly near ragged canvas tents extending in misaligned rows from two sides of the house. They watched him silently and with expressionless faces.

They climbed the shaky steps to the porch, and Reuben opened a door and roughly yanked him into the house where his nostrils were struck by the pungent odor of mold, stale sweat and urine, and other offensive smells he could not identify. Reuben shoved Myles into a dusky room lighted only by whatever shafts of sunlight filtered through the filthy curtains. He was then pressed down into a straight-back chair facing a warped dining table, behind which sat two men and a white-haired woman. Reuben took a chair next to a younger man so they all sat in something of a semi-circle in front of Myles.

The council, Myles figured. The black-haired, finely attired man with moustache and goatee had to be Lord Cyrus. Myles placed the man in his early fifties. The woman, sitting to his right was no doubt Agatha. He had first tagged her as an old woman, but the white hair had skewed his opinion. Her skin was remarkably wrinkle-free and nearly flawless, obviously a person who had not spent much time laboring in the harsh sun. Her black dress might have caused Gina to characterize her as a witch, assuming that was her usual attire. Reuben, he had already met, and the fair-haired young man's pale blue eyes matched Agatha's, but unlike the others, his expression carried no malice. To the contrary, he seemed uneasy, and Myles thought he would probably prefer to be elsewhere.

He was barely aware he was under the scrutiny of the council members as he fell into his lawyer's habit of evaluating the people across the table. There was no question in his mind that this man Cyrus was in charge and that the other members were present to ratify whatever he decided.

Confirming Myles's conclusion, Cyrus Crabbe spoke, "Good afternoon, Mister Locke. You are seated before the council of Peace Commune. I am known as Lord Cyrus, and I am the chairman of this body. You have been summoned here to answer questions and discuss matters of great importance. Your very life may depend upon your answers and cooperation. Do you understand?"

"Yes," Myles said. "It is already quite clear to me that I have no independent control over my future." In his mind, however, he did not believe the words he mouthed.

"You are our guest here for the moment, but you have become a problem."

"I must say I find your guest accommodations unusual, but I do not see how my presence is a problem for you. I certainly did not ask to be brought here. If you wish me to vacate the premises, I will be pleased to do so."

"Spare me your sarcasm, Locke. You should have been dealt with like the sheriff's deputy, but Brother Reuben foolishly deemed you to be of some value to the commune, and he and Timothy here brought you to the commune. At first, I agreed you might be of some value as a hostage if the law accused some of our people of the killing of the woman known as Granny Gray Owl. But, instead, you have compounded the problem."

"I have done nothing of my own volition."

"What were you doing at Miss Gray Owl's property? It seems strange that you would be accompanying a deputy sheriff to the property."

"I was her attorney. Now I am executor of her estate. I rode out with the deputy for the purpose of inspecting the land and determining whether there were personal items that might be salvaged."

"Does your so-called salvage include the woman's gold bullion?"

"I have no idea what you are talking about."

"It was well known that Miss Gray Owl did not produce and sell her medicines and potions because of her benevolent heart. She charged steep prices for that crap. She sure as hell didn't live up that loot, so she stashed it some place. Damned old greedy Indian capitalist."

And a smart capitalist, too, Myles thought, investing her money very wisely. "I would know nothing about that."

"I think you do. You were going out to her place to find that gold, and the helpful shyster would see that the money got lost on the way to her estate."

"There was no gold. I am certain of it." He found himself curious now about what Granny had buried in the goat pen.

"If you tell us how to find it, you might buy your way out of your little predicament."

"As I said, I know nothing about any gold, and I am confident she had none. I had never even heard the rumors you mentioned."

"Well, you ponder the gold business a little more. It is likely your only way out of Peace Commune. Now, I want to talk about some snoopers that came by this morning."

"Snoopers?"

"Yes. Two men mounted on Appaloosas and a slender woman who sat tall in the saddle of a blue roan. One of the men, who thought he was their leader, was dressed like something of a dandy. The quiet man was the local vet I've seen around Medicine Wheel. Looked like your younger self. Do you happen to know those folks?"

He was being tested. No point in lying. "I think you know very well who they are. I assume you encountered my sons and a rancher named Kirsten Cavelle."

"I've heard of the woman. She pretty much owns the town of Medicine Wheel, I'm told. Tough bitch. But she sure draws a man's attention."

Myles saw Agatha flinch at the latter remark. "If you're smart, you will release me and the little girl before they return. They are not persons to be taken lightly."

"Oh, I don't take them lightly. Our time here is up. Time to move on. It's not the first time."

"You have a lot of people to move out. You won't be able to outrun the county lawmen."

"Most of our people will be staying behind."

There was something final and ominous in the way the so-called Lord Cyrus made the declaration that made Myles's blood run cold. "If you are leaving anyway, why not release us before you depart. It won't affect your head start."

"Now come on, Mister Law Wrangler. You have be-come a witness. I have already as much as told you who killed the deputy, and you saw Timothy and Reuben at the scene. And I am telling you now that I did in the old lady myself. She forced me to by her resistance. There, you have my confession. What do you think of that?"

"I think you have decided you are not going to risk letting me live." He was surprised at how calmly he responded, but he supposed it was because he had accepted a few moments after he woke up in hell that a death sentence had been ordered by someone.

"If your family or the law shows up here with a large force before we escape, we may need to put you on exhibit alive to prove that an attack imperils your life. Of course, you are a dead man anyway. And my plan is for you to die in the fires of hell." He laughed. "A bit of humor. When the time comes, you will see what I mean."

Myles said nothing but met Cyrus Crabbe's dark glare and fixed his eyes on the man until Crabbe turned his head away.

Crabbe said, "It appears Mister Locke has no useful information for us. Even if he knows where the old squaw kept her gold, there is no way we could retrieve it now. Do any of the council members have questions?" He did not wait for a response. "Hearing none, Reuben, escort the man back to hell."

Chapter 22

KIRSTEN ROAMED THE commune property again with her telescope, giving special attention to the compound. There was still no sign of anyone giving chase to Marty or starting a search for the missing guard.

She turned to the girl, who sat in the grass wearing the ragged top of a dress and some baggy under-bloomers with legs cut off so they scarcely covered her buttocks. "I don't have any clothing for you, Marty, but I do have some moccasins in my saddlebags. Your feet will probably swim in them, but walking on this rough, rocky ground might not be so difficult."

"I've lived mostly barefoot so my feet are tough, but that would still be nice."

Kirsten got up and retrieved the moccasins and a half-full bottle of horse liniment from her saddlebags, handing the soft doeskin footwear to Marty before she set down the bottle and knelt to check the compound with her telescope again. Then, watching the girl slip her feet into the moccasins, she asked, "Too big?"

"They're fine. Feel nice."

"Good. Now, you and I are going to have a long talk about this commune and try to figure out how we can help these people. But first, I want to know about those raw welts on the back of your thighs."

"I was punished for an act of rebellion. I pointed out to members that while others in the commune were near starvation and reduced to wearing rags, Cyrus and his council ate well and always wore the finest clothing. Someone informed Cyrus I was spreading messages of insurrection. I was sentenced to a public whipping—stripped naked and my wrists and ankles tied to a post while Cyrus administered sixteen lashes with his bullwhip. The worst are on my back."

"Why sixteen?"

"One for each year of my age."

"I have some liniment I would like to put on your wounds. Would you permit me?"

"I guess so. I took the whipping a week ago, but the lashes are still sore and festering."

Marty immodestly pulled up the back of what remained of her dress while Kirsten administered the liniment. The whip slashes were scabbed in places, pus-filled in others, and she took her handkerchief to press away the discharge before applying the medication. She noted the crisscrossing of old scars on Marty's back. "This whipping wasn't your first, was it?"

"No. Two other times. I was branded a troublemaker after my mother disappeared. And I refused to go to any man's bed. Cyrus wanted me, and when I fought him off, he kicked me out of the house and assigned me to a tent with Gina. I was informed a few days ago that I would become one of the common wives, and that if I refused, I would be taken to the whipping post again. I could escape this duty by returning to the house and being one of Cyrus's exclusive women as my mother had been. His son, Timothy, delivered the message, but he wanted me for himself. I could tell. Timothy is Cyrus's son by Agatha, who is his principal wife and bosses the other women. It's strange. She does not seem to be bothered by Cyrus sleeping with whatever woman he chooses. She and Timothy both sit on the council with Cyrus and his lackey, Reuben. I don't think Timothy is evil like the others and sometimes I felt sorry for him. Anyway, I was not going to be a common wife and was planning to get out one way or another before I heard their plans for the people in the commune."

"And the people tolerate this treatment of others?"

"I think their spirits are crushed. Many people attracted to the commune were those who had failed at life on the outside. Some were lazy and were enticed by the idea of living off someone else's labor. Others had fallen on hard times because of just plain bad luck and were drawn by the idea of working for the common good. My mother brought me here because my father had come to a terrible end from tetanus. She had worked with him on our little farm, but we could not handle it without him. She sold the farm, but it took most of the money to pay the mortgage. Cyrus learned of our plight and appeared at our door the day we were packing to leave the farmhouse. He invited us to join the folks at Peace Commune. It sounded like heaven, and my mother accepted."

"I wonder how he chose you and your mother?"

"I don't know, but I must tell you that my mother was a beautiful woman. In due time Cyrus had his way with her, and she became one of his exclusive women for almost a year before she told me we were going to leave the commune. She had come to hate it there and called herself nothing but a whore. She and I worked hard in the fields, but many had excuses for not sharing in the labor. Sore backs. Too busy. That sort of thing. But we received nothing extra for our work. Everything supposedly went into a common pot to be shared equally by all—after Cyrus skimmed the council's share off the top. My mother said that Cyrus and those who did not work were no more than thieves stealing from our labor."

"But your mother was Cyrus's lover."

"That's why she called herself a whore. She shared his bed to get extra food and a room in the big house and so we could be warm in winter. Unfortunately, the arrangement required she had to be available whenever Cyrus summoned her. But it also kept her from being a common wife. She feared that if something happened to her, I would end up being a common wife or whore for Cyrus, and that is why she told him we were going to leave. Of course, something happened to her anyway."

"I'm sorry. Perhaps, we can learn what became of her."

"She's not alive. I know that. If she had escaped the commune, she would have gone to the law to free me. She would not have abandoned me in that place."

"You mentioned 'common wife' several times. Just what is that?"

"It's a commune. So everybody shares. Right? The women are available to all the men who select which of the women they wish to bed on any given night. If more than one man desires the same woman, they draw lots or arm wrestle or play some other little game to determine who gets the woman for that night. Of course, there are no common men. The women have no similar right of selection. It seems to always work out that way, doesn't it? The men make the choices."

Kirsten replied. "Not always. Only if the women allow it. I make my own choices. And it seems to me, you made yours."

"It is interesting how the leaders of the commune are above the rules for everybody else. They do not choose from the pool of common wives. Cyrus had the right to choose as many exclusive women as he wished—he usually had three besides Agatha. They had to treat him well, for if he was displeased, they would be expelled and become a part of the pool of common wives."

"How many people occupy the commune?" Kirsten asked.

"I've never really counted. Let me think." She paused for several minutes. "There are twelve men. That includes Lord Cyrus and Timothy. Seventeen women besides Agatha."

"And children?"

"Lots. More than thirty. Mostly under ten years old."

"Do you have school teachers? How do they learn?"

"No teachers. And they don't want them to learn to read and write. I was lucky, I learned those things before we came to the commune. But I want to learn more. I loved to read, but books are not allowed there. Not even the Bible."

"Then it is not a religious group?"

"No. Lord Cyrus and Agatha quote the Bible sometimes if there are words that serve their purposes. But there's not a lot of praying and church services and things like that."

"That's about half the number of people who live in Medicine Wheel. How do they feed everybody? There is not enough land to support that many people, even if they were farming it or grazing it efficiently—which, of course, they are not."

"I think they mostly steal what they need. It's not enough because everybody's going hungry—except the council. Our remaining cattle were slaughtered this spring. Lord Cyrus and Reuben and Timothy came back with a mule and a bunch of goats a few nights back. They were butchered that night, and we had a big party. Everything was butchered, including the mule, and fires were built all over the place for a big roast. The people will have enough to eat from that for a short spell. When things get too bad again, the men will go out and then come back with a few calves, sometimes a big steer. They hardly ever brought in deer or other wild game. My father used to kill enough wild game for us to eat even in the worst of times. These men aren't much for hunting or doing anything that takes patience and initiative . . . other than steal."

Kirsten said, "Some of the ranchers, including me, have been missing beeves—a calf here, a steer there. Not enough to get too excited about, but a concern. This probably explains it."

"I think they steal about anything that's not tied down when folks are gone from their places. They must steal some money, too, or sell some things they've stolen, because sometimes they'll bring in flour and beans and other foodstuffs they must have purchased some place. But it's never enough to feed folks for long. There are days when there is nothing to eat." Marty shrugged forlornly.

"If the sheriff and a posse of citizens try to enter the commune, will anybody put up a fight?"

"The women won't. Those that are left don't have any fight to them. They're with the commune because they're dependent on the council to live—or they've been made to think they are. Most have children, but they don't even know who the fathers are in many cases. They have come to think they cannot care for themselves, and they don't have any man who assumes personal responsibility for any woman or child. The women see themselves as helpless. I wasn't raised that way, and my mother didn't buy in to it after she understood what was going on, and that's why she's dead. As to putting up a fight, the men are armed with rifles, but I don't see many standing up to defend the commune. Lord Cyrus knows this. That's why he's going to get out of there and leave the others behind to burn."

"Marty, I want you to tell me where everything is at." Kirsten handed the telescope to Marty. "Start with hell. Where exactly is it located? What's the fastest way to get to it?"

Chapter 23

THAD DISMOUNTED IN front of Quincy Belmont's meat processing plant, a modern facility that included a slaughter house, smoke room and ice house attachment. He looked up at the big sign above the entryway of the limestone building: Belmont Meat Enterprises. Quincy was a born entrepreneur who had mustered out of the buffalo soldiers at nearby Fort Riley. A master sergeant who had seen Army service during the War of the Rebellion and, afterward, fighting Comanche on the Staked Plains, he had taken up preaching in the Flint Hills north of Manhattan not far from Medicine Wheel.

He started a small hog farm, recognizing that every man in the Flint Hills fancied himself a cattleman, and there were few sources of pork nearby. His operation quickly grew and prospered, and he constructed a large smoke house on his farm for curing meats he produced from animals that were not sold for breeding or home slaughter. When Kirsten conceived of the Medicine Wheel company town to be located adjacent to a new railroad line extension, Quincy signed on immediately and built a facility that would process both hogs and cattle for shipment to big cities. Nearby Fort Riley was a major customer for his products. He operated the plant with as many as ten employees during busy times. Local ranchers called Medicine Wheel "Little Chicago" because of the livestock marketing center Quincy had established.

The burly Negro businessman was also grandfather to Thad's son, Ned, and Thad and Quincy had become fast friends over the years. Thad had forged strong ties to the Belmont family, notwithstanding the fact he and Serena never married. In fact, Quincy and Rachael's daughter, Elizabeth, who was approaching her eighteenth birthday, worked as an assistant in Thad's office and would be departing in a few weeks to enter the veterinary program at Iowa State Agricultural College. Thad had promised her a position in his practice when she graduated.

Quincy came out the front door with a cowhide folder in his hands before Thad entered the building's front office. Quincy looked like he was wearing his church duds, and Thad wondered if he was on his way to a funeral. Quincy stopped and offered a big smile when he saw Thad and stepped toward him and extended a huge hand, nearly crushing the veterinarian's own. Thad thought if he shook either Cam's or Quincy's hand one more time this day, he would be forced to take a leave from performing surgery till his fingers recovered.

Thad said, "You in a hurry? You look like you're headed for a church affair."

"No, Doc. I'm strolling down the street to chat with my banker about an expansion plan I've got. The banker is near the Almighty in the commerce world, and if you want his money, I figure it's best to dress to show respect."

"Spare me a minute?"

"Sure. What can I do for you?"

Thad told Quincy about Granny Gray Owl's death and their suspicion that Myles Locke was being held hostage at the Peace Commune. "Do you know anything about those folks out at the commune?"

"I've encountered some of them. The one I remember best is a big bearded fella, bigger than me even. Kind of a growly guy. Demanding sort. Till he saw I didn't push easy. Think his name was Reuben. Claimed they were a religious settlement doing God's work, but after I quizzed him some, I decided he wouldn't know a Bible from a Sears and Roebuck catalog."

"What did they want?"

"Any waste cuttings from the meat processing—things we can't sell. Not a market for kidneys and brains hereabouts. We can sell beef livers but not much of the pork livers. Anyway, they looked hard up, and we've got to dump the stuff some place, so we put the waste in barrels in the ice house, and a few of the commune men brought a rickety wagon in once a week to bring back the empties and load up the full barrels. They were regular for about three months but haven't been in for the past three weeks. We've had to start taking the waste to our dump site in the hills. Pretty well gets eaten up by coyotes and buzzards and others of their kind."

"Uncle Thad?"

Thad turned and saw Wrangler riding up behind him. "Wrangler. I thought you were with Kirsten."

"She sent me to tell you what's happened since you left." He told Thad and Quincy about Marty's escape from the commune compound and what she disclosed about possible plans for firing the house to distract others from the council's abandonment of the place.

"Do you believe this girl?"

"Yes, Uncle Thad. She doesn't have any reason to make this up. Kirsten's afraid Gramps will die in the fire, too. She wants you to get the fire equipment and as many volunteers as possible out there as soon as you can. She says there's no easy way to get there. Nearest road is two miles away and you'll need to take the county road from Granny's and go east about three miles till you hit a turn-off that goes north two miles and dead-ends. After that, you cut back northwest cross-country, skirting the canyons. There should be some wagon tracks where folks have got to the road in the past. Kirsten said it's probably the most isolated place in the county and that's why nobody knew what was going on out there. I'm supposed to head for town and find my dad and tell him what's going on."

"Was the sheriff at Granny's yet when you went by there?"

"Nope. And Red was mighty pissed. He said he had work to do and couldn't be sitting on his butt out there all week waiting for Sheriff Sam to get off the chamber pot. Cookie's promised beef stew, biscuits and apple cobbler for supper, so I'd guess he'll hold the crew together for tonight. They'll start wandering off if something doesn't happen by morning though."

"If the sheriff doesn't get his act together by then, we won't be waiting. We'll have to go in without him. If we can get everything in place before then, we'll move in during the night. I'm guessing your dad's in Manhattan right now. Go ahead and try to track him down and let him know what's developed. Tell him I'll get the fire brigade in action, but he might want to round up a few more guns if the sheriff's short of help."

"I'm on my way, Uncle Thad." Wrangler wheeled his horse and soon disappeared into a curtain of dust raised from the street.

Thad turned back to Quincy, who had silently taken in the conversation. "I guess I've got work to do. I'll ride back to the fire hall and ring the bell. I hate to take the time to try to round up those working on the outlying ranches. Some of the volunteers are already at Granny's, but I may be short-handed getting the wagons out there."

"I can see my banker another day. I'll help. Let me go back to the plant. We can hold up the slaughtering, and I'm betting two or three of the boys on that end would gladly help out—especially if I tell them they're still on my pay clock."

"I won't turn down your offer. I have a bad feeling about what's ahead."

"You go on down to the fire hall. I'll be there in fifteen minutes."

Thad was greeted by a tail-wagging Cinder at the fire hall. Her eyes begged for action and escape from the kid hugging her hip. Thad would oblige this time. The Dalmatian might be a critical asset. "Stay girl. I'll be right back."

Thad rushed across the street and entered the clinic, relieved when he found Elizabeth at one of the reception area desks dealing with some paperwork. She looked up and smiled. "Doctor Locke," she said, "I'm so glad you're here. Folks are wanting to set up times for working cattle, and I don't know what to tell them."

"Any other problems?"

"None I haven't been able to handle so far."

That covered a lot of territory because he knew Elizabeth's skills already exceeded that of most vets, who had little formal training and were essentially self-designated. There were very few veterinary schools in the country and generally no licensing regulations. He had even considered taking her into the practice in a few years based upon her apprenticeship, but he wanted her to be the finest she could be and not limited to his approaches to animal health care. "We'll have to hold off a few days before making appointments, and I'll count on you to take care of emergencies. You read my note about my missing father?"

"Yes. Have you found him?"

"No, but we know where he's at." Thad quickly explained the dilemma. "I hope to be leaving the fire hall with volunteers within the next hour. I need Cinder. Can you babysit Socks?"

She laughed and got up from her chair. "Sure. She's a sweetheart. I fed them over at the fire hall this morning, and I even coaxed her away from Cinder for a bit. I'll run over and bring her back to the clinic. I'll have to cage her overnight, and she won't like that."

They walked back across the street together. Thad was not unaware that he walked with a striking young woman whose lithe form could not be hidden by her clinic smock. Her tawny skin leaned to her mother's half-blood Seneca-white heritage, and she shared Serena's dark, expressive eyes. For that matter, she might have been Serena's near replica if she were not a good half-foot taller than her older sister. They certainly did not share personalities, Thad thought, as Elizabeth was far more ebullient and outgoing than her more serious, often reserved, older sister.

When they reached the fire hall, Thad was pleased to see that Socks went to Elizabeth without protest. Cinder's eyes, however, followed her ward worriedly as the young veterinary assistant returned to the clinic, toting the kid in her arms.

Two regular volunteers, Angel Cortez and Dutch Schwartz, arrived at the hall and raced immediately to the stable area to begin hitching the teams to the Studebaker and pump wagon. They were both young men in their early twenties who operated Kirsten Cavelle's grist mill up the street, both hard-working and reliable.

When Quincy showed up with the O'Hara brothers, Frank and Fremont, the teams had pulled the wagons out of the fire hall, supplies were loaded, and they were ready to pull out. The O'Haras, who appeared to be Africans of undiluted blood, were both members of Quincy's congregation and lived with their families in employee homes on Quincy's farm, helping in his swine-breeding and feeding operations when not working at the processing business in Medicine Wheel. Since the newcomers were mounted, Angel and Dutch stepped up into the pump wagon and Studebaker, respectively, and took the reins. Cinder jumped into the Studebaker, and Thad mounted Inkblot and rode away, signaling the others to follow.

Chapter 24

IT UPSET CAMERON Locke that Sheriff Sam Mallery had not returned by the time he checked in at Granny's place. He headed for Manhattan, expecting to encounter the sheriff and some deputized citizens on the main road. He did not, and his annoyance turned to anger. By the time he tied his horse in front of the sheriff's office mid-afternoon he had worked himself into a fury. He reminded himself that his temper was dynamite with a short fuse and stood outside for several minutes, composing himself before he opened the door and stepped in.

Sheriff Mallery was leaning back in his chair, feet propped on his desk when Cam walked in. He set his coffee mug on the desk, removed his feet and sat up in the chair when he saw Cam. "Well, howdy, Cam," he said, rendering his politician's phony smile.

"I sent in a rider with a message. I thought you would be on your way by now."

The sheriff stood up. "Well, yes. I was just getting ready to ride out that way. I've been waiting for some more help. And my other two deputies should be back soon. They're out making an arrest between here and Fort Riley. Some old fart made off with his neighbor's butcher hog."

"I think you've got your priorities damn twisted. You've got a deputy killed and a missing citizen, and you're sending your help after a pig thief. Meanwhile, you sit here on your fat ass drinking coffee."

The sheriff's face turned beet-red. "Now see here, Cam. I ain't going to put up with that kind of talk. I'm the law, and I'm entitled to respect."

"You won't be the law after the next election if I can do anything about it."

"I'm tired of putting up with threats from you and that Cavelle bitch."

"I don't have time to argue with you, Mallery. Here's what you're going to do. You are going to round up Judge Wallace and hold him in his office till I get there. We need a warrant to search a place called Peace Commune. I'll explain it all to the judge. Understand?"

The sheriff's hands were trembling, and Cam could not tell if the source was fear or rage. Maybe a mix of both. He didn't care.

Mallery said, "You got a nasty temper and bad attitude, Cam. But I'll cut you some slack because I know you're upset about your father. I'll meet you at the judge's office in the courthouse."

"And be ready to ride because, deputies or not, we're heading to Granny's when we get that warrant, and I want you there when we serve it on those cutthroats at the commune."

"But it will be dark."

"You should have thought of that earlier. Bring your bedroll."

Later, when Cam walked out of the courthouse with the sheriff, who now had a warrant in hand, he was surprised to see his son, Wrangler, waiting at the hitching post.

"Wrangler," Cam said as he approached his son, "I left you with Kirsten. What are you doing here?"

"A lot has been happening since you left, Pop. Kirsten sent me to tell you, and I saw your stallion hitched here, so I figured I would wait." He told Cam and the sheriff about Marty's escape and the council's plan to set fire to the compound to cover their own exit.

"It seems we need to move in as soon as possible," Cam said.

"It'll be dark as a bat's cave," the sheriff said. "Cloud cover moving in. Won't even be any moonlight."

"It will be just as dark for those bastards," Cam said. "I'll give this some thought."

Chapter 25

THAD WANTED TO speak with Cam before he moved the fire-fighting equipment near the Peace Commune, so he led the volunteers and the new recruits to the encampment at Granny's place. Red and the other volunteers had already been fed off the chuck wagon, and Cam's two cowhands had eaten and departed earlier to relieve Kirsten, who was expected back soon.

Cookie quickly fetched more beans and made up biscuit dough for feeding the new arrivals. By the time he was ready to serve up the meal, Kirsten rode into camp with a half-dressed young woman snugged to her back and clinging to her waist to keep from sliding off the big gelding. This had to be Marty, the girl escapee Wrangler spoke about. Thad walked out to meet Kirsten and reached up and took Marty's hands and helped her slide off the horse.

"I'm Thad," he said, "Kirsten's, uh, friend."

Marty grinned impishly. "She's told me about you—mostly good things."

That reply was sufficiently vague to keep him off balance. "Well, we can talk later. Supper's ready. Why don't you two check in with Cookie so he sets aside something for you to eat? After supper, we'll talk."

Kirsten dismounted. "We'll do that, and then we can dig through my knapsack and see if we can find something else for Marty to wear. I've got a pair of denims and an old shirt. She'll probably have to roll up the pantlegs and tie the waist with a rope. She's on the petite side. But we'll put something together. Can't have her running around half-naked among all these horny cowboys."

Kirsten handed Thad the horse's reins and took off with a bewildered Marty in tow. The girl probably had no idea how safe she was in Kirsten's custody. On second thought, he decided, Marty had already seen what Kirsten could do with a gun.

He was about to give up on Cam when his older brother showed up with the sheriff and Wrangler. When Cookie saw the new arrivals, he hollered, "Get them stragglers over to the chuck wagon. This is the last call. Anybody else turns up, they go hungry."

After everyone had eaten, Cam collected Thad, Kirsten, Marty, Red, and Sheriff Mallery to set up a plan. It was clear to Thad that that the sheriff had been relegated to a mere observer's role and that Cam had taken charge of the mission.

They sat in a circle around one of the small fires as they talked. Cam asked Marty, "Young lady, tell me straight. Do you really think this Lord Cyrus would burn up the place with all those people in the house?"

"He would, and he wouldn't lose a minute's sleep over it."

"Can you find the place where they've got my father?"

"Yes. I know exactly where it's at. But he's in kind of a pit, and the trapdoor would be padlocked."

"Are you willing to go back in there with Kirsten and Thad to lead them to the spot?"

Marty's eyes took on the look of a startled doe, and her lips quivered. She looked to Kirsten for an answer, but none was forthcoming. Then she seemed to summon her resolve, setting her chin, tilting her head toward Cam, and meeting his gaze. "Yes, I can do this."

Cam turned to Kirsten. "Kirsten, you know this part of the county better than anybody. Thad says you will have to take the road as far as it goes with the fire wagons. After that, you must get the things overland on ground that will take wheels. And this will have to be done quietly so any guards aren't alerted. We want to choose the time for the party."

"You're talking four or five hours. I could walk it in less than one-third that time without the wagons and equipment. Under darkness—and staying behind the hills—we could get within quarter of a mile of the entrance without being seen or heard."

"From what Marty says, it doesn't appear we will be facing overwhelming numbers, perhaps eight or nine who can handle a rifle. Probably not many experienced fighters in the bunch. They will have a guard posted at the gate. That's fine. I suppose we'll have to take him out because that is likely the best wagon entrance. But, first, my boys and I will take our wire cutters and open the fences around the perimeter of the farm. We'll slip in one of the openings nearest the compound. After we take out the sentry, I want Marty to lead Kirsten and Thad through one of the openings we cut out and try to find the judge and get him out of there. Maybe I'll send Wrangler with you."

Thad asked, "Do you plan to strike before sunrise?"

"Yes. I can't believe they're crazy enough to set fire to that place, but, just in case, we need to try to head it off."

Red Holiday interjected. "We've got to head off any fire. Dry as it's been, it could get to the grass and then the timber in the canyon in no time, and then God knows how you stop it. It wouldn't take much wind to carry it all the way to Medicine Wheel."

"We'll try to head it off, if the idiots really intend to set a fire."

Thad thought Cam sounded skeptical of the fire threat. He did not share his brother's skepticism.

Sheriff Mallery, whose silence and scowling face evidenced his displeasure with Cam's assumption of authority, interrupted. "We got a warrant for a search. It's got to be served before we start anything."

Cam snapped, "You can serve it on a corpse, Sam. You had your chance. My father is in that place, and I'm getting him out of there. On second thought, why don't you ride up to that guard at the gate and give him your piece of paper while we're taking down barbed wire."

"Alone?"

"We've got things to do. And we don't have time for you to wait for those deputies who are rounding up a notorious pig rustler. Looks like it's up to you. Go ahead."

"Well, I won't be a part of this unlawful raid you're instigating. You could be disbarred for this, you know."

"I would love to explain to the state newspapers why we had to do this on our own—why innocents had to die because of your inaction."

The sheriff stepped back, the sullen look on his face signaling his defeat. Thad had no doubt if things worked out Sam Mallery would weasel his way to the front of the line to take credit. But he had covered his ass in preparation for failure.

Cam said, "Red, I'd like two of your volunteers with rifles they aren't afraid to use to ride with me and my two cowhands. The others can go with the wagons. We'll meet up with the two men keeping watch, and that should give us plenty of guns. Thad and Kirsten's crew can ride with you till they split off to sneak into the compound. The volunteer brigade can move toward the main gate when they hear gunfire just before sunup. Thad's crew shouldn't wait. They'll need to go in on foot ahead of the ruckus to make their search. I'm hoping they find the judge and get him loose before all hell breaks loose. But if not, they'll have to make their own decisions."

Red said, "We'd just as well move out. If we don't run into trouble, we can grab a little shuteye when we get to where we're going."

Cam said, "Any objections to what I've laid out?"

No one spoke up, and Thad had no better strategy to offer even if he had been up to an argument with his bull-headed sibling.

Chapter 26

REUBEN GRABBED THE neck of Myles's shirt and half-dragged him back to the pit prison. While his jailkeeper unlocked the padlock, Myles took in the surroundings. A stack of hay nearby, but not much. A half dozen horses, including his rented animal, in stalls on the other side. His mount, although nothing special, was the healthiest-looking of the occupants. The others seemed almost skeletal, and they had raw sores on their backs and hips. They obviously were starving and suffering from neglect. When they had walked with Reuben to the council meeting, he had noticed ample grass on the surrounding prairie. Why didn't they graze the horses there or harvest the grass for hay? Lazy or ignorant? Aside from the cruelty to the horses, Myles could summon up nothing but contempt for men who were too stupid to appreciate the economic value of caring properly for these creatures they depended upon for transportation and carrying out day-to-day work.

He noticed a rusty pitchfork stuck in the hay pile and wondered if he could reach it while Reuben fussed with the padlock. His answer came when Reuben sighed heavily and lumbered to his feet and pulled what appeared to be an old Navy Colt from the holster on his gun belt. Was his execution coming? Was he going to be dropped into hell to ultimately join the other bones there? And what about poor Gina?

"Pick up the ladder and drop it down there," Reuben growled, "and get your ass back to hell."

Myles obeyed, but when he climbed down the ladder, he noticed the hinges on the trapdoor, in contrast to the metal clasp and lock, were made of old, worn leather. He filed the information in his head for future reference, although, at that instant, he could not see how it mattered to him. When he stepped off onto the stone floor, the ladder was abruptly pulled up and the trapdoor slammed shut.

Myles turned to look for Gina, but his eyes had not yet adjusted to the darkness, and he could not see her. Then he heard her soft whimpering near the wall where he had left her earlier. He knelt and crawled toward the sound of her sobs. "Gina, it's Myles Locke. I'm back, and I am going to come sit beside you."

"I'm here," came a tiny voice. "But my head hurts, and I'm scared."

"It's okay to be scared, sweetheart," he said when he neared her and began to make out her shadowy form. He scooted up next to her and leaned back against the wall, stretching out his arm and pulling her close. He did not consider himself very good with children, and he sometimes worried that his own children, when small, had found him cold and distant. He loved them dearly but knew his reserved and hesitant nature sometimes hid the depth of his feelings. This poor girl touched his heart, and he was determined to console and protect her.

She clutched him now, pressing her head against his ribs, and he caressed her hair soothingly, speaking softly, "I will stay with you now, Gina. I will not leave you. I will take care of you. I promise." Could he keep this promise? He would, or he would die in the effort. Suddenly, this innocent little girl became his cause.

Gina spoke, still clinging to Myles. "I found the bones. Are they my mom's and Nathaniel's?"

"I don't know, dear. I really don't know." But he had no reason to think otherwise.

Ron Schwab

"They are, I think. But it's not really my mom any-more. She's in heaven. That's what Marty said. Her mom is, too. I feel her here, but she's just visiting."

Myles had no answer to Gina's words, so he just con-tinued to hold her as he tried to sort things out. His sons evidently suspected he was at this place, whatever it was. They would show up eventually. He just needed to keep Gina safe until that time. He was not a violent man. He had been too old for military service during the War of the Rebellion, and he could not recall ever striking any-one in anger. But he wished desperately he had a weap-on—anything: a rifle or pistol, even a knife or club.

The skeletal remains. Could he salvage a weapon from the bones? He looked down at the girl in his arms. Gina had calmed now. He hated to release her, but he had a thought. "Sweetheart," he said, "can you stay right here a minute? I want to see if I can find something. I'll be right back."

"I guess so," she said uncertainly.

Myles slipped away from her and got up and stepped over to the opposite wall of the room, where the clusters of bones lay. He knelt and feathered his fingers over the cold remains. He touched a smooth, narrow piece of something and then felt several more. A rib cage, he decided. He latched onto a bone fragment and yanked.

Something snapped and the piece broke free. He rubbed the hard surface. Smooth and a sharp end, perhaps seven or eight inches long but curved. He might sharpen it a bit by rubbing it on stone, but it wouldn't slice anything—like the leather hinges, which he could not reach anyway. He shrugged and, clutching his find in his hand, returned to Gina's side, taking care not to reveal the rib bone as he placed it on the floor within reach.

Gina leaned against him as he sat there, again clutching him and fastened to him in a way that bore deeply into his soul. Soon she surrendered to sleep, and her head dropped into his lap. He gently traced his fingertips over the lump on the side of her forehead where she had been pistol-whipped. It did not seem terribly swollen. Certainly his own wound dwarfed it. She had not complained again about her headache, so he liked to think his presence had distracted her from the pain.

He reached out with his free hand and clasped the stolen rib bone, feeling a bit ghoulish for having appropriated a piece of human remains. He commenced honing it on the stone floor, rubbing it back and forth, trying to sharpen the point and smooth sharp edges. He supposed he was not accomplishing all that much in the construction of his dubious weapon, but it was something of a distraction from his and Gina's plight. He found him-

Ron Schwab

self growing drowsy, and then he released the rib bone and his head slumped as he joined Gina in the world of dreams.

Chapter 27

THE RUTTED COUNTY road faithfully followed the steep, up-down contours of the surrounding hills, and on several occasions Thad worried whether the single team could pull the loaded Studebaker up the incline. Once the wagon got hung up on the road center where the ruts burrowed deep and a blunt-headed limestone boulder jutted up in the middle. It had taken a half dozen volunteers to help hoist the wagon axles over the offending hump.

After the public road dead-ended, the wagon trek to an overlook near the Peace Commune had been challenging and time-consuming. The pitch black shroud over the Flint Hills had obliterated any prior access routes that might have been carved by use into the limestone surface lying only a few inches below the grass-carpeted layer of soil. They finally picked up a trail after completing three-fourths of their journey. But Kirsten's four- or five-hour estimate had turned into nearly six hours.

Regardless, it was still several hours before sunrise, and prior to the brigade's departure, Cam had informed Thad and Kirsten the barbed wire would be cut as soon as he met up with his watch-team near the commune. They would not take the gate guard out until a half hour before sunrise, at which time they would move into the compound

Thad and Kirsten were asked to locate the judge and, first, move him away from any conflict. Then, if they were able, they would join in the assault and help round up the commune occupants. Wrangler and Marty were to lead the judge to the horses and safety. Thad was fully aware that such plans rarely played out according to script and tried to prepare himself for any ad-libbing that might be required.

Thad and his little group decided to ride their horses and stake the mounts outside the gap in the fence. If they entered from the east, he was confident they could remain outside the guard's line of vision. Thad borrowed a horse for the judge from one of the volunteers, who took a place on the pump wagon seat. Thad removed a shovel and axe and several canvas tarps from the Studebaker wagon and lashed them to the extra horse's saddle. As an afterthought, before he mounted his Appaloosa, he called Cinder to his side. "You come with us, girl."

Kirsten knew the terrain best so he nodded for her to take the lead as Wrangler and Marty fell in behind, and they rode away from the cluster of wagons and mounted volunteers. He noticed that a gentle breeze had graduated to brisk wind during their night ride and knew that did not bode well if a fire should break out. They circled northeasterly, staying with low ground until they approached the barbed-wire fence. They dismounted and, leading the horses, began walking the fence line. Shortly, they came to a gap between two posts where the wire had been cut away. Cam or one of his cowhands had been here. They stepped through the opening and stopped to discuss their next move.

They could not see the ranch buildings from this spot, but the compound sat on only a quarter section of land. The building site was located not far from the northeast corner of the one hundred sixty-acre tract so Thad figured it could be no more than a quarter-mile distant.

"Kirsten," he said, "you've been studying the place. Where is the barn in relation to the other buildings?"

"East of the house and a bit to the north. There are some other small outbuildings, but the barn dwarfs them. It's a huge barn. I assume it includes a stable. There are several steel watering tanks in a corral on the east side, and I could see a water pump and windmill near one of the tanks. I didn't see any cattle or other livestock. We're in the right spot to get to it without anyone in the house spotting us. Of course, with it being this dark, we could probably walk into the barnyard without being seen."

Abruptly, a line of flames erupted on the horizon, casting light on the building compound.

"Oh, shit," Kirsten yelled, "they are going to burn the place down."

Cinder began dancing nervously and barking, signaling they should be heading for the blaze.

"They're burning the tent homes," Marty said. "That would be the north row." No sooner had she spoken than another line of flames burst up directly south of the other.

"Let's get moving," Thad said. "Our job is to get to the barn. The brigade should be on the move."

Chapter 28

CAM AND HIS four riders were biding time just inside the east fence line when the orange, waving blazes rose from the compound. He had hoped Thad would locate their father and set him free before they launched an assault on Cyrus Crabbe and his ragtag outfit. He told Charlie, his grizzled foreman, "Wait here, but if I'm not back when the volunteers come through the gate, ride in with them and give cover." He wheeled his big stallion in the direction of the gate, aware the guard would be alert now. Regardless, he had to clear the way for the fire brigade to get through.

As he approached the gate, he saw that the guard was facing him with rifle raised to fire. In that instant he realized the backdrop of light from the compound flames outlined his form as a perfect target. Too late now. He could only hope the guy was a lousy shot. He tapped the stallion's flanks with his boots and charged ahead, his Army Colt readied in his right hand. How many times had he done this, leading a charge against Yankee infantry as a young Confederate captain? And they had never touched him. That was what he was thinking when he heard the defender's rifle crack twice and felt a hammer blow to his chest that nearly launched him from his saddle. The stallion raced on, almost upon the rifleman now.

The man jumped out of the way, and before he could raise his rifle again, Cam squeezed the trigger of his own weapon twice, and his adversary dropped the rifle and crumpled to his knees before falling facedown on the hard ground. Cam dismounted, his head spinning, and stumbled to the gate and pulled off the wire loop that snugged it to the post and swung it open. Then he collapsed. There was pain in his chest, but it was not that terrible. He struggled to understand how he could survive four years of bloody combat and then let some failed clodhopper bring him down just a few miles from home. Blackness descended before he could figure it out.

Chapter 29

MYLES SMELLED SMOKE. And he thought he might have heard distant gunshots. He could not make out what they were saying, but frantic voices sifted through the cracks in the ceiling. He could see no light through the fissures in the boards so he assumed it was still nighttime, which made little difference to him. Now he heard someone rattling the padlock on the trapdoor above. He tensed. The door opened. He saw a shadowy form, but it appeared too slight for the man called Reuben.

The visitor spoke. "I'm going to lower the ladder, old man. You are to come with me."

"I'm not leaving without the girl."

"She stays. Lord Cyrus said so."

"Who are you?"

"Not that it makes any difference, I'm Timothy Crabbe."

"Why do you want me to come out, Timothy? Where are you taking me?"

"I can't say. But you will die if you stay here. You'll be roasted like a pig on a spit."

"I won't go unless I know where you are taking me. And Gina comes out with me."

"You are a hostage, old man. The council is riding out of this place. But we're taking you with us as a bargaining chip if we get cornered some place. It's your only chance to get out of here alive."

"But sooner or later you'll kill me anyway."

"Maybe. Maybe not. But this way you got a chance."

"But Gina stays behind?"

"That's right."

Gina had awakened now and was sitting upright beside Myles. "Please, Mister Myles. Don't make me stay here alone. Don't leave me," she whimpered.

"I will not," Myles whispered. "I promise. I will not leave you." He called to Timothy, "Very well, young man. You win. Lower the ladder."

"Now you're sounding sensible. Didn't think you was that stupid, being a law wrangler and all."

Myles could hear Timothy Crabbe wrestling with the ladder as he positioned it to the trapdoor opening to slide it into the pit. Shortly, he heard the scraping of wood against stone as the ladder slid downward. "Stay here," he softly admonished Gina. "I must do something. I am not leaving you."

"Promise?"

"Promise." He would die first, he vowed, knowing that indeed might very well happen. He stood up and moved under the opening, feeling for the approaching ladder. He grasped the bottom rung, which was on a level with his chest. "I've got it," he said. Timothy released the ladder, and Myles tugged sharply, stepping back, as he pulled the entire ladder into the pit, the top clattering along the wall before it crashed onto the stone floor.

"What are you doing you old fool? Set that ladder back up and get your scrawny ass out of there."

Myles moved away from the opening and returned to Gina, sitting down beside her, placing his arm about her shoulder and pulling her to him. He responded to Timothy, "I changed my mind. I am not coming out."

"You are insane, Locke. You'll burn down there. We're setting fires now. This barn and the house are next. Smell this. I'm pouring kerosene on the hay now. I'm lighting it before I walk out of here. One last chance. Are you coming out?"

Timothy was not bluffing. Myles could smell the pungent odor of lamp oil. "Can I bring the girl?"

"No girl."

He didn't trust Timothy to keep his word anyway. Once they came out, either he or one of his father's loyalists would eventually kill them both. And Gina would just be drug through more mental anguish on her path to death. Regardless, nothing would take him away from the little girl. "I'm not coming out."

The trapdoor slammed down, shaking the board ceiling and dropping puffs of dust into the pit. "Okay, old man. Burn in hell."

Myles could hear muffled sounds coming from the barn above and then the whinnying of horses. If they were deserting the place, they would need horses, of course. A retreat for the council members and other anointed elite was obviously in progress.

"Are we going to die in hell, Mister Myles?" Strangely, Gina's voice sounded more curious than fearful. Perhaps his nearness gave her comfort. It suddenly occurred to him that the arrangement was reciprocal. The girl gave him someone to care about besides himself.

His thoughts went to his own children and what they meant to him and how in many ways, to his thinking, he had failed them. He had been obsessed with the legal problems of his clients, often working seven days a week and sometimes long into the night, convincing himself he must pursue his work to put bread on the table for his family. "The law is a jealous mistress," his own lawyer father had warned him. And he wondered now if his children would have been better off with more father and less bread.

And he had virtually surrendered parenthood of the twins, Thad and Hannah, to their aunt and uncle, who had given them the time and love that he thought now should have come from their father. Thad seemed to bear no grudges over his decision, but Hannah had confronted him about what she perceived as his abandonment before she departed for Wyoming to carve out her legal career there. After ten years she still never responded to his monthly letters. He relied upon Thad to keep him posted on the happenings in her life. He had not seen or spoken to her directly in at least five years when she had made her last visit to Manhattan. Estranged. Yes, that was the legal word to define their relationship. As his arm hugged the little girl beside him, he thought he had never held his own daughter like this. And he never would. He remembered something else his father had told him: When a lawyer is on his deathbed, his last thought will never be, "I wish I had spent more time at the office." Of course, by then repentance is too late. At that last thought, Myles was yanked from his reverie by the unmistakable, acrid odor of smoke.

Chapter 30

SOMETHING HAD GONE wrong. Thad and his party raced toward the barn in search of his father, but he had to assume they were on their own now. The fires, which he had always considered speculation, had started well before sunrise, although it made sense now. Those sleeping in the house would be caught by surprise, unable to resist and less likely to escape. And he could see little fires being ignited at the base of the house

He had heard gunshots coming from the direction of the gate, but he saw no sign of Cam and his riders moving toward the building site. He assumed Red and the brigade members had seen the flames and were on their way. He could make out men scurrying around the exterior of the house, several with torches in hand. The area was quickly becoming well-lighted by the flames, and now he caught sight of a cluster of skittish horses tied to a rope line between two posts, presumably mounts readied for an escape. He was tempted to make a dash for the horses and cut them loose, but it would be a forty- to fifty-yard run, and there was no cover if he should be seen. He had to try to find his father first. As they approached the barn, he and the others crouched behind one of the water tanks to re-group.

"Okay, Marty," Thad said. "Where do we find this so-called hell pit in the barn?"

"I spent two days in it after one of my whippings. I'll never forget it. Dark and cold and damp. There are somebody's bones and two skulls down there. I think it is Gina's mom and her lover. The only entry is from this side—the south. There is a door at the other end, but it's nailed shut. The pit is in the northwest corner, so it's closer to that door. Big doors, so you can get a wagon in. They both move on a slider-thing."

"Okay. Here's what we're going to do. Wrangler, you and Marty stay here. Kirsten and I are going to go in the barn and find your Grandpa. Have your Winchester ready in case you need to cover us. If we can find him and get him out, we'll come back here, and you and Marty can take him to where we left the horses while we try to help the others."

"We can do that, Uncle Thad."

"Cinder, come," Thad said to the Dalmatian, and the dog fell in at his heels.

Thad and Kirsten rushed toward the barn, Thad toting the big fire axe in one hand and his rifle in the other. Kirsten had left her rifle with Marty, who insisted she could handle the weapon, having hunted and killed rabbits and other small game for food on her parents' farm. Kirsten's holstered Colt rested on her hip, though, and Thad suspected she was more than ready to use it.

When they reached the barn door, he was startled when it slid open and billowing smoke followed a bent-over, coughing and hacking man through the narrow opening. He appeared to be a young man, seemingly unaware of their presence until Thad spoke. "Stop right where you are, mister. We're looking for Myles Locke. Take us to him now."

The man straightened and jerked his head from side to side as if looking for help. Evidently seeing none, he turned back to Thad. "Never heard of the man."

Thad handed Kirsten his Winchester and raised the axe. "Take us to Myles Locke or I split your skull."

The young man's eyes widened in terror and he turned away and started to run, before he plummeted to the ground with Cinder's jaws clamped to his ankle. "Good girl, Cinder," Thad said, as he brought the blunt end of the axe down on the man's head with a sickening crunch. It was not his intent to kill, but he didn't have time to ponder the man's condition.

Kirsten yelled from the partially-opened barn door. "Thad, the smoke seems to be coming from the back of the barn, and flames are climbing the wall at that end. We can't get through the smoke."

He hated to give the command, but he pointed to the opening, "Cinder, seek." The dog shot through the doorway.

"We'll try the other way," he said. "I'll chop through the door."

He grabbed the rifle from Kirsten and took off running with Kirsten following a step behind. When they reached the rear door, he saw smoke and flames escaping through gaps in the wood siding. He feared they were too late, but he set the rifle down and began swinging the big axe frantically at the door. It was his bad luck that the door surrendered only splinters with each strike. He could not imagine someone had wasted good oak on a barn door, a wood that got only stronger and harder as the years passed.

"Thad," Kirsten screamed. "Listen."

He froze the axe mid-swing. Then he heard the frantic barking. Cinder. His heart sunk. She could not be that far from the door. She would die in that inferno. But she was telling him she had found something. His attack on the door turned into a crazed frenzy.

Chapter 31

MYLES COULD HEAR the snapping of flames above, and the odor of smoke was unmistakable. He had no doubt that Timothy Crabbe had made good on his threat to burn them in hell. Strangely, he thought, the smoke had not yet creeped into the pit, and for now, at least, they had an air supply. Then it occurred to him that smoke generally rose to an air source, so unless the smoke had no other escape, they, perhaps, had some time. But eventually walls and barn roof would cave in and fall upon the ceiling of their prison and the fire would eat its way through and roast or suffocate them.

"Mister Myles, are we going to die?" Gina asked in a voice he could barely hear. She was nearly paralyzed by fear. She had her arms clutched around his neck now and had moved onto his lap.

"No," he replied. "We will get out of here. Someone will come."

"Will God save us?"

Myles' religious outlook carried as much doubt as faith, but he said, "Yes, do you know how to pray?"

"Mommy taught me. I pray for her every day."

"Then pray now. Ask for God's help." He did not know how else to deal with the child. Would the truth be better? Should he tell her that within thirty minutes they would be choked by smoke and ravaged by flames? He decided when the time came, he would cover her body with his, so, perhaps, the inhalation of smoke would mercifully claim her life before the flames chewed at her flesh.

Abruptly, he heard what sounded like hammering or knocking on a wall, rapid and continuous. Then there was something at the trapdoor. A repeated, fast scratching or scraping, like tool against wood. Had Timothy reconsidered? Had he decided to release them? "Who is there?" he yelled. "Timothy?"

The reply was frantic barking. A dog? What was a dog doing here? Then he heard voices. He lifted Gina from his lap and set her down. "I must find out who is there," he said.

"I think it's God. I have been praying."

If there was help, he was more than willing to give God the credit. Myles stood up and yelled, "We're down here. Two of us. A little girl and me."

"Myles, it's Kirsten. Thad and I are up here. We've got to move quickly. The fire is spreading through the barn. The door is padlocked."

"The hinges. The hinges are leather. And I have a ladder down here."

Kirsten called out Thad's name, and an axe blade came through the door seam. Taking out one hinge and then a second, and, momentarily, the trapdoor flipped open.

"Your ladder," Kirsten yelled.

He reached for the ladder and started to hoist it to the opening, but he found himself struggling and dropped it. When he had taken it from Timothy, he had just pulled the bottom rung back, and it had collapsed into the pit. He grabbed the ladder again in an attempt to wrestle it up but then stepped back when he saw a pair of legs dangling from the opening. The body dropped into the pit, and he recognized his son.

Thad immediately sprung up and grabbed the ladder rungs and pushed the top of the ladder upwards. Kirsten hollered, "Got it," as she positioned the ladder against the stone rim above the pit.

"Help Gina first," Myles said.

"No, Dad. You go on up and help Kirsten steady the ladder. I'll bring your friend." He turned to Gina and scooped the little girl into his arms. Myles returned the pilfered rib bone to its nest, vowing to see the remains properly buried if he survived. He climbed the ladder on shaky legs and disappeared through the trapdoor opening. Thad, with Gina hugged to his chest and arms clinging to his neck, scaled the ladder rungs quickly. Myles took the girl when they emerged, clutching her hand, as they all stood near the edge of the pit seeking out an escape route.

"Thad, the door opening's cut off by flames," Kirsten said, her voice hoarse now from the smoke. "We can't go back that way. There's no way out."

Cinder commenced barking and turned and started back toward the south end of the barn. "Cinder wants us to follow," Thad said. Picking up his axe in one hand, he reached for Gina with his other and took her from his father and lifted her again to his chest, and, instinctively, her arms wrapped around his neck. "Dad, you and Kirsten stay close."

Myles felt Kirsten's hand grip his wrist. She tugged him ahead, trailing Thad. He could hear the dog barking behind a curtain of smoke. He glanced upward, and through the gray haze, he could make out orange-red flames eating at the rafters and dancing along the underside of the barn's roof. It appeared hopeless. He started coughing now, the smoke finding its way into his lungs, and he could not breathe without taking in more smoke. He fought back panic when he heard Kirsten's voice and felt her pulling him down. "On the floor. Keep your head down. Crawl."

He went to his knees and found air. Kirsten remained beside him, her fingers clasping his belt now, as if trying to half-carry him forward. They crawled together for what seemed an hour but was likely no more than a few minutes. The dog's barking was louder now, and they turned a corner into what was evidently a horse's stall. Gina stood in the corner, her fingers clinging to the collar of the black and white spotted dog at her side.

Thad was facing the exterior wall, readying his axe. Then Myles realized what his son was doing. There was a splintered hole near the floor, where the wood had apparently rotted. The hole would admit nothing larger than a rabbit or a cat, but Thad was obviously preparing to enlarge it. Thad swung the axe, and the rotted wood caved easily. Then Myles heard the cracking of wood above him and saw a section of the roof caving, raining red-hot coals as it gave way. The axe hit the wall twice more, leaving an opening large enough to squeeze through.

"Dad, hurry," Thad said. "Take Gina." It didn't seem right somehow that a man with the fewest potential remaining years of a lifetime should go first, but the delay of debate made less sense. He grabbed Gina's hand, pulling her away from the dog just an instant before timbers tumbled from the roof, crashing down on the animal. A yelp. And then silence interrupted by Thad's yelling, "Dad. Go. Go."

Myles went, shoving Gina to the floor and pushing her through the hole and then squeezing clumsily through himself. He had not clambered to his feet yet when Kirsten emerged with flames leaping from the back of her shirt. She immediately tumbled over onto her back rolling in the dirt and grass to smother the flames. Myles hurried to her assistance and knelt beside her, brushing away the remaining smoking cinders. She sat up and looked around. "Thad. Where's Thad?"

"He's not out yet."

"Damn him. He's trying to reach Cinder. I know he is." She crawled to the opening in the barn wall. "Thad. Come on, the roof is collapsing. You can't save her," she screamed. "Thad, do you hear me? Get the hell out."

Chapter 32

THE BARN WAS an oven now, caving-in piece by piece. The saving grace was that smoke was escaping through the ragged cavities in the roof, leaving a bit more air in the expanse above the barn's dirt floor. Thad stumbled over the simmering rubble, ignoring Kirsten's screams from outside the building. "Cinder," he called, "Cinder, baby."

He heard a whimper from beneath a pile of smoking timbers in the corner of the stall's remains, and he rushed to the sound, yanking and tearing away the charred stumps with his axe till he found the Dalmatian, her hip pinned to the floor by a heavy support post that had crashed on her. She lifted her head and looked at him, the agony in her eyes breaking his heart. He sought unburned handholds on the smoldering timber and grasped it with his hands. It took all his strength to lift and pull the timber away. His profession necessitated a resilient stomach, but what he found beneath sickened him. The hair on the Dalmatian's left hip had been seared off to the skin, leaving a patch of raw and charred meat like a beefsteak grilled over an open fire. The leg below had somehow been ripped open from just above her toes to the top of her thigh, as if she had been sliced with a cleaver. Blood pumped from a severed artery.

She would bleed out in minutes, he thought, and he pulled a handkerchief from his back pocket, wrapped it around the leg where thigh joined hip and tightened it until the bleeding ebbed. Then he leaned over and worked his arms under the dog's body, and cradling her in his arms, stood up. He staggered a bit in the process. Cinder was large for a female of her breed, weighing over fifty pounds, he guessed.

"Thad, the place is falling apart. Get Cinder over here."

Only then did he see Kirsten, who was half way back through the exit hole. He moved toward her and put Cinder down. "Help me get her out of here."

Between the two, they maneuvered Cinder through the opening barely ahead of the fire that was starting to consume the stall. They all moved a good distance from the barn before Thad took inventory of his situation. Cinder lay on the ground, motionless now. He knelt and checked her over and found her pulse strong but her breathing raspy. The tourniquet had stopped the serious bleeding. He just hoped he wasn't too late.

Little Gina spoke for the first time. "Is the puppy dead?"

"No, sweetheart," Thad replied. Not yet, he thought.

"I'll pray for her."

"Me, too," Myles said. "She saved our lives. That's the least I can do. I just hope we haven't used up our prayers for one day."

Kirsten said, "Thad. The bastards are burning the house."

He suddenly realized he had left his Winchester behind the barn. "I hate to attract their attention, but start firing your Colt. Maybe that will alert the folks in the house. Then we make a beeline for the stock tank."

Thad bent down and lifted Cinder again and headed toward the tank where Wrangler and Marty were hunkered down. Myles followed with his hand clasped tightly to Gina's. Kirsten fired three shots in the air and quickly joined them. The sun teased with its first glow on the horizon, signaling its rays would make an appearance soon. But already forms were changing into something more than shadows. When they swung around to the front of the burning barn, he noticed the young man was still prostrate on the ground, either unconscious or dead. He was not a threat anytime soon.

Wrangler and Marty came out to meet them as they neared the stock tank, and Marty immediately ran to Gina, spreading her arms to receive the little girl when she broke away from Myles to greet her friend. "Thank God, Gina, you're safe. I was so afraid for you."

"Mister Myles was with me, and we asked God to help us. He sent Cinder."

"I'm glad you are both okay."

Thad placed the Dalmatian down behind the stock tank. It was the best he could do for the moment. There were others to consider. He looked toward the commune's horses—or to where he thought they had been hitched. But the horses were gone. "Did the council escape? The horses aren't there."

"Nah, Uncle Thad. I cut them loose. It was Marty's idea, and she covered me. But they never even noticed. With the fires going, those horses took off like a nest of hornets was on their tails."

It was either a brave or foolish deed, possibly both with a comely young woman to encourage a sixteen-year-old's daring. Now what to do about the people in the house? His question was partially answered when he heard the clanging of the fire bells from the wagons. He looked toward the gate. They appeared to have stopped there, but the mounted volunteers rode on, joined soon by the others. He assumed the new riders were Cam and his crew, but he could not make out the Appaloosa stallion. Then the wagons started to move up the road again. "Wrangler, I think it would make the most sense now for you to get our horses and bring them up here. Do you think you could handle that many?"

"I'll help," Marty said too quickly.

Well, he would let Cam and Pilar deal with the budding romance. "Okay, go ahead." The two raced off together but stopped when Thad called to the young woman. "Marty. We might need one of the rifles. Would you leave your Winchester here?" She rushed back and handed him the rifle and dashed off to join her new friend. She swam in Kirsten's extra shirt and trousers, and they gave her something of a hobo look, but he guessed that Wrangler's imagination wiped away any ambiguities.

He turned the rifle over to his father. "Dad, I hope you don't need this, but I want you and Gina to stay here with Cinder. Maybe Gina can talk to her and try to console her. They seemed to hit it off. I can't help her anymore until things settle down."

"We'll hole up here, and I won't hesitate to use the gun on these people if it comes to that." Gina was already sitting on the ground, back against the tank with Cinder's head in her lap. The Dalmatian licked weakly at the girl's hand, and Thad found this encouraging. At least she was still conscious.

Thad held onto his axe, and he and Kirsten circled the collapsing barn to recover the Winchester and shovel that had been abandoned earlier, but both lay beneath a stack of smoldering, still-burning rubble. They headed in the direction of the house and heard the crash of windows breaking as they neared. Hopefully, the occupants would escape before the house was consumed by flames.

At least four men were breaking for the spot where they had tied the horses, which he realized now had been out of their view because of the darkness and smoke from the burning tents. When the men arrived at the place, however, they scanned the scene in stunned silence for a moment and then scattered, taking cover behind the privy and a nearby chicken coop while they pondered their dilemma.

"Cover me," Thad said to Kirsten as he headed for the house, determined to break in doors and windows to free its occupants. He could see that some were hoisting small children out of main floor windows, but breaking windows on the second floor signaled that some must be trapped upstairs.

Chapter 33

KIRSTEN FOLLOWED THAD to the house, stopping and swinging around intermittently with her Colt at ready to be certain they were not being pursued. Dawn was now starting to light up the compound grounds, and she caught a glimpse of a man stepping around the corner of the outhouse with rifle raised to fire. She sent a few wild shots in his direction, and he dived for cover. These were not seasoned gunmen, she decided, and it would not take much to keep them at bay. But she had not seen anyone who looked like Cyrus Crabbe. And where was the woman Marty said was his wife? And the big man called Reuben?

The fire wagons pulled into the yard now, and she could hear Red's booming voice issuing orders. Thad's axe had chewed away the door hinges, and when he pushed the door aside, a flood of women and small children poured out of the house.

One of the volunteers maneuvered the mules and pump wagon near the house, and two men jumped off the wagon and began rolling out the hose. Two others prepared to work the pump. A man was unloading canvas coats and distributing the thick leather fire hats with buckets, axes, and other gear from the Studebaker. It appeared Red was forming a bucket brigade at the well outside the house, which was engulfed in flames now.

Her eyes returned to the Studebaker to a man who appeared to be kneeling in the wagon bed over something. Then she saw Quincy Belmont's unmistakable bulllike frame rushing her way. He approached her, nearly breathless.

"Kirsten," he said. "Where's Thad?"

"Well, he's right here," she said as she turned toward the empty doorway. "Or he was. Oh shit. He went into the house. Quincy, I don't know what's got into him. He's lost his mind."

She ran through the doorway with Quincy right behind her. Curtains were ablaze, and flames were climbing the walls, smoke forming a dark cloud-like cover over the ceiling. She saw Thad framed in an enclosed stairway climbing to the second floor with axe in hand, his exit cut off now by flames crawling along the floor at the bottom of the stairway and eating their way up the stairs. "Thad," she screamed. "Get out. Now."

He turned and yelled back. "Tarps. Ropes. Ladder. To the windows."

She understood instantly. He was going to try to get the entrapped children out the second-story windows. Either run a rope line or drop the children onto the canvas tarps held by volunteers, or both. This was a tall house, and she questioned whether the ladder would extend to the second-floor windows. "Did you hear him, Quincy? We've got to tell Red. We need to save pump wagon water and use it beneath the windows."

"I heard him. I wanted to tell him his brother might be dying. But let's move."

His words stunned her for a moment, but Quincy tugged on her arm. This time she followed Quincy, instinctively set on doing what Thad requested. But her heart and soul were with him on the second floor. She could not lose him now. The prospect of loss told her what she had always known deep-down. She could never love another man like she loved Thaddeus Jacob Locke.

Chapter 34

SMOKE WAS CLIMBING the stairway behind him, but it had not yet filled the hallway. There were four doors leading off the filthy hall, all bedrooms he assumed. He could hear voices, children crying and screaming behind the doors. He tested a doorknob. Of course, it was locked. Three swings of the axe, and it flew open. Four children, three no more than six years old, he guessed, the other a prepubescent girl. "Stay," he yelled. There was no time for coddling.

He raced to the other rooms, repeating the process, checking windows for the best exit and deciding the southeast room was best. No exterior flames below it yet. He broke out the windows clearing away glass and obstacles, while two of the older children collected the others and herded them to the room. He slammed the door behind them and directed his two ten to twelve-year-old assistants to stuff parts of sheets or other fabric under and around the door to seal the smoke out. He counted thirteen children in all, the youngest could not be more than three years old.

Looking out the opening that had been a window, he saw that volunteers were congregated below, and the hose was sending water from the pump wagon to soak the walls below the window. The tarps he asked for were spread out on the ground, ready for use. Quincy held a rope with a lead weight anchored to one end and heaved it toward the open window. The weight sailed through, carrying the rope-end with it and landed with a thump on the floor. Thad grabbed the rope and pulled the entire rope through the opening and quickly tied the weighted end with a bowline knot about his waist. The loop would hold fast but not slip and tighten about his torso.

Thad then made a smaller loop in the other end and slipped it under the arms of one of the older girls, a skinny blonde urchin with straight tangled hair and a dirty face streaked from her tears. These kids were all skinny, outright skeletal. At this moment, their underweight bodies might be helpful.

The girl looked at him anxiously. "What's your name, sweets?" he asked.

"Nancy," she stuttered.

"You just hold onto this rope, Nancy, and I'm going to lower you to the ground. Don't worry if your hands slip, the loop under your arms will hold you, and I won't let go."

"I'm afraid of high places."

"Just walk over to the window. Close your eyes and hold on to the rope. I'll do the rest."

She obeyed, bit her lower lip and closed her eyes as Thad lifted her over the window sill and began letting her down. He saw several of the volunteers extending the ladder and pushing it upward against the side of the house. As he feared, it was not going to reach the window ledge. And he could hear flames crackling in the hallway now as they gnawed at the walls, and puffs of smoke were beginning to creep around the door. He would never get them all out in time, and the little ones would not be able to deal with the rope. Nonetheless, working his way down by size, when he pulled the rope back in, he cinched another girl in the crude harness. When he sent her over the ledge, he saw that the ladder was set up now, reaching almost within two feet of the window, leaving just enough room to manipulate the rope. Kirsten was climbing toward him. Where were the men? Then it occurred to him, she would weigh the least of the volunteers and was likely the most agile. By the time he started lowering one of the boys with the rope, Kirsten was positioned below the window. Beneath her was Angel Cortez, the wiry volunteer, who would not weigh much more than Kirsten.

Kirsten extended her arm. "Grab my wrist. Pull me up so I can help with the little ones."

There was no time to debate. He leaned out the window and latched on to her wrist, and she grasped his. He hoisted her off the ladder rung, and she was suspended in the air for just a moment before she grabbed the window sill with her other hand, and with Thad's help, clambered over the ledge and into the room with an undignified landing on her butt.

Kirsten scrambled up off the floor and picked up the smallest child, a little girl, while Thad prepared another boy for the rope elevator. The girl shrieked with fear as Kirsten held her out the window and lowered her into Angel's arms below. Angel passed the child to Red, who had positioned himself next, and Red lowered the child to another volunteer. Soon they got into a rhythm with the relay, and Kirsten had removed eight of the small children by the time Thad finished with the last of the larger ones.

The door was ablaze now, and smoke was filling the room. "We've got to get out," Thad said. "Now. I'll lower you back to the ladder."

"No time. I'm jumping." She stepped onto the window ledge and leaped like she expected to soar to the earth.

Thad rushed to the window opening, fearing he might see Kirsten's inert body sprawled on the ground. Instead, she was bouncing off a tarp stretched out by six volunteers. She smiled up at him and waved at him, gesturing at him to follow. Crazy Kirsten. He was not about to leap, but he crawled out the window, locking his fingertips on ledge, and lowering his body its full length to reduce the distance of his drop. Then he pushed away from the wall and released his grip, plummeting to a soft landing on the outstretched tarp. He rolled off the tarp, knowing his drop was not as graceful as Kirsten's exit. When he stood on shaky legs, he almost fell over when Kirsten flew into his arms and planted a lingering kiss on his lips. The bystanders broke out in cheers and applause.

He could feel the heat of embarrassment spreading down his neck, as Kirsten whispered, "I love you Thaddeus Locke, but you've got to stop flirting with Miss Danger. I can't take much more of this."

Chapter 35

KIRSTEN STARTED TO tell Thad about Cam, but a grim-faced Quincy approached and broke the news before she had a chance. "Thad, I hate to carry bad news, but Cam's been shot. Bleeding bad, but I've tried to staunch it with some rags."

"Where is he?"

"In the Studebaker wagon."

"I keep an emergency medical bag under the seat. I'll head over to the wagon. Would you two check on Dad? See how Cinder's doing? Maybe you can move everybody over by the wagon. Dad and Wrangler need to know about this."

As they walked toward the stock tanks, Kirsten's eyes turned back to the house. Red had the volunteers focusing on containment now. Stopping the house fire would be a hopeless effort, and Red had apparently decided to let it burn to the ground. Priority was to keep the fire from spreading to the surrounding tallgrass prairie. Two volunteers were wetting down the ground around the burning house with the pump wagon hose, but the water tank would likely dry out soon. They would need to move the wagon nearer the well to refill. Fortunately, the wind had died down this morning, but sparks from a fire could still drift a good distance.

What were they going to do with all these people, mostly women and children, wandering about the farmyard aimlessly with bewildered expressions on their faces? She wondered if someone else had made their decisions for so long they had lost their capacities to think and cope. Old Charlie and Cam's Circle L hands had apparently corralled most of the gun-toting resistors. Four men sat on the ground near a towering cotttonwood tree, hands clasped over their heads, but she saw no sign of the two Crabbes and their lackey, Reuben. She did not think the commune leaders could have escaped on horseback unless they had other mounts secreted some place. Would Cyrus and Agatha leave without their son? Probably.

Passing the south side of the barn, she noticed that Timothy Crabbe was moving now, tossing his head back and forth, trying to struggle upright, fighting like a turtle on its back. "I don't think he's going any place soon," Kirsten remarked, "but we'd better find somebody to keep an eye on him."

The problem was solved when Sheriff Sam Mallery loped his mount into the yard. Accompanied by a chubby, wide-eyed young deputy, Mallery surveyed the scene with a satisfied smile on his face, looking very much like a man in charge now. He saw Kirsten and Quincy and nudged his horse in their direction and then reined in and dismounted. The deputy remained saddled, his eyes fixed on the moaning man stretched out on the ground.

"Well, Miss Cavelle, it appears we've got things pretty well under control here," Mallery said.

"If you exclude yourself from 'we,' Sheriff. The volunteers and Cam Locke's crew have dealt with most of the problems. Myles Locke is safe now, and nobody died in the fire. Cam took a bullet, and Thad's with him now. This worthless bastard on the ground is guilty of attempted murder and may have been involved in killing Deputy Stewart and Granny. He's your responsibility now, Mallery."

The sheriff walked over to Timothy Crabbe and gave him a sharp kick with the toe of his boot, but the young man, already writhing from the pain in his skull, didn't seem to notice. "He don't seem too dangerous," Mallery said.

"No," Kirsten replied, "I think you can handle this one."

The sheriff didn't miss her sarcasm and shot her a miffed look.

"Homer," Mallery said, nodding to his deputy. "You stay here and keep an eye on this one while I take a look around."

"Sheriff," Kirsten said. "The leader, Cyrus Crabbe, and his right-hand man haven't turned up, and I'd guess they've either done the killing or directed it. Crabbe's wife is likely with them. I think they're still nearby so you might want to watch your back."

The sheriff tossed nervous glances over his shoulders. "We may need some help rounding them up."

"Why am I not surprised?" Kirsten said, unable to resist another dig.

Mallery missed her sarcasm this time. "What about all these women and kids milling around out here, and who are those yahoos over by the tree?"

"The men were the best Crabbe could come up with for gunmen it appears. Mostly they fathered the kids, but I'm not sure anybody knows which ones. I don't think the women are guilty of any crimes, but they and the kids are half-starved, and you will need to figure out what to do about them."

"If they ain't killed nobody, it don't seem they're my worry. They're on their own."

She was not going to argue with the callous fool about this. She and Thad would come up with something. "Let's go, Quincy," she said, and turned and walked away.

As they strolled toward the water tanks, Quincy remarked, "I get the notion you don't like Sam Mallery much."

"It shows that much? I think the word is 'contempt.' Yes, the man is contemptible. And when he opens his mouth, he belches bull farts."

Quincy chuckled. "I'm going to try and stay in your good graces, Kirsten."

"Oh, you are, Quincy. I need you to pray for me. You're my only telegraph line to the Lord."

"I'll pray for you ma'am. And whilst I'm at it, I'll toss a good word in for Doc Locke. I think he might need the help more."

Chapter 36

KIRSTEN WAS PLEASED to find that Wrangler and Marty had returned with the horses, but she was less enthused by the sight of Marty's hand clinging to his and the boy obviously relishing it. This relationship was going to require a bit of icy water tossed on it. She guessed they were both romantic novices, but nature had a way of changing that too quickly. But why should she even care? The girl was making her feel maternal, and this was a foreign experience to her.

She informed the others about Cam's gunshot wound. Wrangler and Myles immediately departed with their two horses for the Studebaker wagon. Marty and Gina remained with Kirsten and Quincy while they tended to Cinder, fashioning a stretcher-sling from a saddle blanket. The Dalmatian was obviously in pain, but the tourniquet had abated any serious blood flow. Kirsten decided to take the dog to the wagon to join Thad's other patient.

Kirsten set Gina in Inkblot's saddle and asked Marty to take the horse's reins and those of the other two horses and follow Kirsten and Quincy as they carried Cinder on the blanket. When they reached the wagon, she saw Thad kneeling in the wagon beside his brother. Cam's deathly-pale face alarmed her, but he was conscious, if groggy and only semi-alert. Thad had a pair of scissors in his hand and was cutting away Cam's white shirt, leaving a blood-soaked, ragged patch of the garment covering the wound. Wrangler and Myles stood next to the wagon with fingers clasped on the sideboards while they watched Thad work on the wounded son-father.

"Can we get Cinder in the wagon?" Kirsten asked as they approached. The rear of the wagon bed was blocked by Cam's prone form and Thad, without speaking, pointed to a vacant spot near the front of the wagon. Kirsten and Quincy swung the dog over the sideboard and lowered her and the blanket softly onto the wagon bed.

Thad straightened his back and leaned back, supporting himself against the sideboard. "I just read about this, but I was skeptical."

"What are you talking about?" Kirsten asked.

"Just a few months ago I read an article by a Doctor Goodfellow on the impenetrability of silk. He recited case studies where a bullet striking silk did not penetrate the fabric but carried the silk with it, often altering the destination. In one instance a bullet struck a silk handkerchief and entered the body where it should have struck the heart, but the silk apparently diverted its course, and the bullet bypassed the vital organ and lodged in shoulder muscle. How many cattlemen would be wearing a silk shirt on the job?"

"Nobody but Cameron Locke."

"And it appears the bullet entered between his ribs and carried part of the shirt with it. That high up it should have been a lung shot, but I would expect more bleeding, and his breathing is steady."

Cam mumbled, "Are you making fun of my wardrobe?"

"Far from it, big brother. It may have saved your life. But we need to get you to a physician who can get that slug out."

"You're a trained doctor. You do it."

"But I don't have the facilities, and physicians avoid working on family members beyond immediate emergency care."

"Don't give me that bullshit. I want you to do whatever needs doing. And do you know how long it will take to get me to Manhattan?"

Kirsten decided to intervene. "Thad, do you have the instruments at your clinic to remove the bullet?"

"Of course."

"Let's take him there."

"It will still take hours on that road we came in on, but I don't want to enter the wound without probes and forceps, so I guess we don't have any choice. But time's important."

Kirsten saw Red Holiday walking toward the wagon and waved at him to hurry.

"What is it Kirsten?" Red asked. "How's Cam?"

"He needs surgery, and we've got to get him to Thad's vet clinic fast. Can you free up a few men to go over to the canyon west of the place and cut poles for a travois?"

"Well, I don't know why not. We're just watching the place burn out now. You can take the wagon, if you want."

"Takes too long. We can get him to Medicine Wheel cross-country in a long hour, no more than two. And I want a travois for Cinder, too. She's in a bad way."

He turned and started to rush away to recruit his logging crew when Kirsten stopped him. "And Red, something else?"

He paused. "Yeah?"

"We need to send somebody back to Granny's to tell Cookie to get the chuck wagon over here."

"He ain't going to like that. And there's no way he can feed all these people if that's what you're thinking."

"My north pasture borders Granny's. Send a few of Cam's boys to cut out a steer to kill and butcher. Just caution them to leave the heifers alone. There ought to be plenty of fire to roast beef on the place. If everybody gets off their butts, we can at least have supper for these folks tonight. Buy some time while we figure out what to do with them."

"Anything else, ma'am?"

Red's tone signaled he was reaching his limit on taking orders. He was accustomed to giving them, but so was she, so she understood. "No, Red. I didn't mean to be so bossy. I appreciate your taking charge of this. I'll ride out with the wounded and get out of your hair."

Red surrendered a smile and nodded. There were few better men, and she did not want to antagonize him further.

Chapter 37

T HAD DECIDED THAT despite his misgivings about Kirsten's undebatable suggestion, the travois transportation had turned into the perfect solution. They had been gone little more than an hour when she led them over a rise above Medicine Wheel. It should take no more than thirty minutes to negotiate the winding deer trail to the thriving village.

"Wrangler," he said. "Could you ride ahead and alert Elizabeth at the clinic. Tell her we're coming in and what happened. Let her know we're going to be doing surgery there and that I need her to get things ready. She'll know what to do."

"Sure, Uncle Thad, we can do that."

He rode out with Marty astride behind him with her arms wrapped around his waist, which the boy appeared to be savoring. He noticed that Kirsten gave a disapproving frown as Wrangler swung his Appaloosa past her. They had doubled-up riders so as not to deplete the horse supply for the commune workers. Gina shared his father's horse, and Cam's stallion, led by Thad, pulled his owner's travois. Cinder's small travois was anchored to Kirsten's mount. Kirsten had been adamant that Marty join them, and, strangely, his father had refused to leave without Gina in tow. More complications to sort out.

Cinder lay on her pole travois without complaint, lifting her head from time to time to look back at him, pleadingly it seemed. He could see the pain in her eyes, and it broke his heart to think he would likely be required to amputate her leg to have any hope of saving her life. Cam, on the other hand, had not been a silent patient. He was half out of his head but howled at every bump and jostling of the travois over the rocky slopes and yelled a string of obscenities when a wave of pain swept over him. At least Cam was conscious, and Thad found that reassuring.

Quincy had remained with the volunteers and Sheriff Mallery to assist with the search for the Crabbes and Reuben. The missing council members were nowhere near the top of Thad's list of concerns right now. His thoughts were focused on the surgeries he would be performing soon.

When they arrived at the Medicine Wheel vet clinic, Elizabeth Belmont was waiting with Wrangler and Marty outside the front entrance. They hurried out to meet them, and Elizabeth promptly moved to Cam's side, grasping his hand and holding it while Thad and Wrangler unhitched the travois from Cam's Appaloosa. Then Kirsten and Myles dismounted and stepped over and grabbed the other ends of the travois, and the four carried Cam into the clinic.

Elizabeth reported, "I prepared the canine surgical table and shoved one of the instrument cabinets against one end for his feet. I knew he wouldn't fit on the table."

Thad said, "That should work fine, Elizabeth."

They carried Cam into the surgery room and hoisted the travois onto the steel-sheathed table. After untying the ropes that bound Cam to the travois, Thad and Elizabeth dismantled the travois piece by piece, easing the poles and sticks away from the patient's body. While Thad and his young assistant prepared for surgery, Kirsten and Wrangler retrieved Cinder and brought her travois in and set it down in a corner of the room. Thad peeled off his filthy, sweat-soaked shirt and washed up in one of three big pots of hot water Elizabeth had boiled in preparation for the surgery. Then he donned a white surgical coat he had pulled from a closet and joined the young woman at Cam's side.

As they stripped Cam's clothing away, cutting his shirt off in pieces, Cam protested. "If you're going to lay me out bare-ass naked, do we need an audience?"

Thad had forgotten about the entourage during his preoccupation with the medical tasks facing him. "Elizabeth and I will take care of Cam. Kirsten, I know you planned to order supplies sent out to those people at the commune and then go back out there. Could you send word to Vedette that Dad is okay? I don't know how to go about it, but I was thinking some of the churches could get involved in helping those homeless folks."

"I'll send a rider into Manhattan to inform Vedette. She's a faithful church goer. Maybe she would know some folks who could get things moving. Of course, Quincy's got a congregation, so he might be able to recruit some help. We've got to notify Pilar about Cam, too. Perhaps Wrangler could ride over to their place and fetch his mother. I'll see what I can do about these other matters before I head back out to the commune."

Thad said, "Marty, would you sit with Cinder and try to keep her calm until I can get to her?"

"Yes, sir. I can do that."

"And, Dad, would you mind waiting with Gina in the reception room? You'll be the first to know when we're finished here."

Gina had been watching wide-eyed, her small hand clutched in Myles's hand, and he started to lead her from the room and then stopped. "Kirsten?"

"Yes, Myles?"

"Would you be sure to let Vedette know I'll be bringing home a young guest with me?"

Kirsten smiled. "Certainly. That should give her something else to ponder."

The room cleared quickly, and by the time Thad turned his attention back to his patient, Elizabeth had covered Cam with a sheet and moved a rolling stand with a tray of instruments into place.

"They've been soaked in carbolic acid," she said.

"Good. Now, I need to have you prepare to administer ether." He spoke to Cam. "We're going to put you under, big brother, so you won't feel anything. But you've got to hold still and not fight Elizabeth when she gives you the anesthetic."

He appeared to only half understand, and he was beginning to writhe in pain, and this worried Thad. Ether was tricky stuff. He used it frequently for small animal

Ron Schwab

anesthesia but would have preferred chloroform for human use.

Elizabeth held a cloth layered with cotton in one hand and a corked can in the other. "Are you going to do this, Doctor Locke?"

"I'm afraid I'll have to hold him down. You've done this on big dogs. Double the quantity for now, and we'll see how that works. Once he's out you'll just have to watch his breathing and add more if he's not staying under. Ready?"

She nodded uncertainly and poured some of the liquid onto the cotton, and then set the can aside and moved the cloth toward Cam's face. Thad bent over the table and pinned his brother's arms down, turning his own head away from the fumes that rose from the cloth, as Elizabeth placed it over Cam's nose and mouth. Cam tossed his head back and forth, trying to escape and would have pushed Elizabeth away if Thad had not pressed him to the table. His weakened state was in some ways fortunate, Thad thought, or he otherwise would never have been able to contain his bigger sibling. Soon, Cam relaxed and dropped off to sleep, and Thad released his grip.

"Excellent, Elizabeth. You seem to have gathered everything I need. You just concentrate on the anesthetic. Ask if you have concerns."

{244}

Thad picked up a probe and forceps and began to explore the wound. He could guess where the slug was not, but the precise location baffled him. He considered tugging on the silk that protruded from the wound to see if he could just dislodge the bullet with the fabric. He spread the flesh about the entry opening to see if he could determine the bullet's course. He was surprised when he saw the slug itself imbedded in tissue just beneath the ribs, still encased in silk. He clasped the fabric and pulled gently, and it emerged easily from the wound, bringing the slug with it. A rivulet of blood followed, but just enough to accomplish cleansing. The procedure was remarkably simple, but he decided he would allow Cam to give credit to the surgeon's skill. He flushed the wound with carbolic acid and stitched it, leaving a small opening for drainage, and then he dressed the wound with gauze and one of Granny Gray Owl's healing salves.

"Elizabeth, you may remove the anesthetic. I just need to figure out where to put him. He's too big for a dog cage. I guess we have a few vacant horse stalls out back."

She gave him a look that signaled she thought he was serious. "Just kidding," he assured her. "But we do need to find a temporary place for him until Pilar gets here. If she doesn't bring a buckboard, she can rent one and a team from the livery, and she and Wrangler can take him home. I can send laudanum for pain, but so long as sepsis doesn't set in, he should be fine. He's strong as a horse."

"There are several straw mattresses in the stable area for owners who stay over or nap while their horse is here for treatment. Could we drag one up here and put him on it? I've got a stack of clean sheets."

"That should work fine. I'll help you get the mattress after I report to my father on Cam's condition. I know he's worrying himself sick."

After informing a greatly relieved Myles that Cam's prognosis was positive, Thad returned to find Cam sitting up on the table and Elizabeth with one hand on his back and the other holding a bucket while he wretched and vomited repeatedly. Ether had that effect on both humans and animals. He asked Elizabeth to stay with the patient while he went back to the stable to retrieve a mattress.

When he returned with the mattress, he dropped it along the wall near Cinder and Marty and checked the Dalmatian quickly, finding her calm and semi-alert. He had wrapped the injured leg with gauze temporarily so he could not evaluate that further until she was on the surgical table. Cam looked better now, and Thad spoke briefly with his brother while his assistant made up the improvised bed.

"You're going to hurt for several months, Cam. Rib injuries are among the worst that way. We need to keep an eye on the wound, and I'll give Pilar instructions for changing the dressings and what to keep a lookout for. But, if you will do what you are told, you should make a nice recovery. Of course, you'll probably disregard my advice and prolong recovery but survive anyway."

"Well, thanks for what you've done. It looks like my horses and I share a doctor."

"I don't expect to handle you as a patient again. Now, let's get you on the mattress so I can tend to my next patient, who hasn't been nearly as noisy about her misery."

When they had Cam settled on his floor hospital bed, Elizabeth and Thad carefully moved Cinder to the surgery table. The dog whimpered but did not resist. Marty asked to remain with the dog, and Thad assigned her to a spot on the opposite side of the table to help steady the patient. Elizabeth would be busy with anesthesia duties again.

First, Thad examined the burns on the dog's hip and concluded they could be dealt with by daily administration of salves. Then he unwrapped the bandages on the shredded leg and scrutinized the injured limb. From the top of the inner thigh to Cinder's ankle, the leg appeared like it had been split by a meat cleaver, exposing bone in places and bloody flesh along the ragged fissure. It would never be the same. She would either be a three-legged cripple or end up with a limp. He had removed dogs' legs before and seen many three-legged dogs and cats that moved amazingly well. He told himself that his objective opinion dictated removal of the leg. But he did not trust his judgment here.

Thad turned to Elizabeth. "What would you do, Elizabeth? Amputate or try to save it?"

She did not hesitate. "Doctor Locke, I have watched you work for two years now. I hope I can be half the surgeon you are someday. You can save the leg. I know you can."

Thad sighed. "Very well. I'll give it a try. Put her out."

Chapter 38

KIRSTEN RETURNED TO Peace Commune just before sunset. She was pleased to see that Cookie had set up his chuck wagon and nearby fires were roasting beef on spits and baking biscuits and beans in Dutch ovens. She figured the beef should be plenty for now, but they would likely need to ration the other foodstuffs for the evening meal. By morning additional supplies should arrive, including huge slabs of bacon and hams from Belmont Meat Enterprises.

The starving women and children were already lined up with tin plates apparently distributed by Cookie and Circle L cowhands, who were assisting with the serving. It was a pathetic sight, she thought. The Flint Hills needed rain, but she hoped storms would hold off till they found lodging for these people.

She noted that since her earlier departure, the house and barn had collapsed and were now burning down to hot coals and smoking rubble. They would have to be watched and the burning controlled through the night to guard against errant sparks setting fire to the tallgrass prairie near the compound, but by morning the threat should have dissipated, and the volunteers could start moving back to Medicine Wheel with the wagons and equipment.

But what about Lord and Lady Crabbe and their loyal knight, Reuben? She saw Quincy striding purposefully in her direction. Perhaps, he carried the answers.

"Any news about Cam?" Quincy called as he neared.

"I didn't stay after we got to the vet clinic. Cam appeared to make the trip without great problems, and Thad seemed calm and confident."

"Thad always seems calm and confident even if something's eating his guts out."

"Yes, that's true enough. He's a damned hard man to read, and it drives me nuts sometimes. Regardless, I think he's in control of Cam's situation. I'm optimistic."

"I wish I could be optimistic about Sheriff Mallery's handling things out here. I always thought he was a nice enough guy, but I think he's just another politician. Smooth as molasses. See if you're going to upset the voters before you decide anything. I offered to help him track the bad guys. In my days as a buffalo soldier, I tracked Comanche. I thought I'd be of some use. He told me he would not need my services and that he had higher priorities."

"And what are his priorities?"

"Talking to newspapers, it appears. A reporter from the Manhattan Nationalist showed up while you were gone, and he's blowing about how he planned this raid and has Granny Gray Owl's and Deputy Stewart's killer in custody. To hear him tell it, these women and kids would've burned up without his intervention. Odd thing is, as soon as the words run out of his mouth, he appears to believe what he said."

"Some natural born liars are like that. Men like Mallery don't have a conscience to struggle with."

"Do you think this Timothy Crabbe is the killer?"

"He might have been in on it. He was possibly present when the killings took place, but Myles told me Cyrus Crabbe admitted to him he killed Granny. Also, it turns out that little Gina was present that night. As near as I can tell, they tried to use her as a decoy to ease their way into Granny's lodge. She's too frightened and confused right now to talk details, but she might have witnessed Granny's murder. I don't think anybody can sort this all out until the leaders are arrested. You say you're a tracker? Why don't you and I go on a hunting trip?"

"Sounds like fun. But the sheriff's not going to like it a bit if a woman and a black man bring in the real killers."

"Do you think I give a shit what the sheriff likes or does not like?"

"Kirsten, I've known you a few years now, and I'm not sure you care what anyone likes when you make up your mind about something. Let's catch some supper and a bit of shuteye and head out at sunrise."

Chapter 39

QUINCY AND KIRSTEN said nothing when they encountered Sheriff Mallery and his deputy after breakfast saddling their mounts and getting ready to return to Manhattan with their trophy prisoner. Timothy Crabbe stood next to a horse, hands tied in front of him. He had a dazed look in his eyes, and the side of his head was swollen and scabbed around an angry cut. So far, he had done nothing but babble, and Kirsten wondered if he would ever regain his sensibilities.

The sheriff obviously was in no hurry to track down the likely killers and had decided a scapegoat would suffice. Kirsten doubted if he would ever get around to serious pursuit.

As they saddled their own horses and strapped on the saddlebags and bedrolls, Kirsten noticed that Quincy had commandeered a double-barreled shotgun and a leather bag of shells from someone. He carried no sidearm other than a sheathed skinning knife. She slipped her Winchester in its saddle scabbard and reflexively feathered her fingers over her holstered Colt before she stepped into the stirrup and swung easily into the saddle. Thad gently teased her sometimes about her grace on a horse, suggesting that she rode like a disciplined ballerina, that horse and rider merged to one the instant she slipped into the saddle. She took it as a compliment and would not deny the pride of horsemanship acquired growing up in Missouri from competition with six older brothers.

"Where do you think we should start, Quincy?" she asked when they were both mounted.

"I suggest we ride the perimeter of the fence line along the quarter section. If they left on foot, there should be sign some place."

"Makes sense."

"Something else. These don't seem like the kind of folks who are going to stay afoot any longer than need be. They also need to get away from this country fast, and it isn't likely they would be above horse stealing. You know these hills better than anybody. Where might these people go to find transportation? I'd guess they've been thieving from the neighbors for a spell and have a good idea who's got what."

As they rode the horses slowly down the trail toward the compound's entrance, Kirsten reviewed her mental map of the ranches north and east of the Peace Commune. West would take the fugitives toward Medicine Wheel, which seemed an unlikely course. Her own homeplace was nearest to the south, and that was five miles as the crow flies. She could think of five possibilities lying within four miles of the commune along likely escape routes. "They've got several options within walking distance. Hills are rugged wherever they go. I've seen the men, and I'm sure they can do the distance. I have no idea about the woman."

"Let's see if we can pick up a trail and narrow it down some."

They started the search of the commune property's border, moving quickly along the south fence line. Riding north, they passed the break in the fence where Kirsten and Thad had entered with their rescue party. The grass was mashed down, and occasional hoofprints appeared on the softer ground, but Quincy found no sign of other travelers who might have exited at this point and broken off in another direction.

They continued north along the east fence line until Quincy reined in his big sorrel gelding. "There," he said, pointing toward the fence.

"What?" Kirsten replied, unable to pick out what had caught her partner's attention.

Quincy dismounted and walked over to the fence. "They crawled under the wire, and somebody got hooked on a barb." He bent over and tugged a tiny piece of cloth off the barb and handed the black fragment to Kirsten.

"Black. Soft. Probably cotton. Came off the woman's dress I'd guess. Didn't keep her fanny down."

"Seems strange, taking off cross country in a dress."

"I've been told more than once real ladies don't wear blue jeans or long pants. A lot of folks—men and women—think that."

Quincy shrugged. "I'm not a fashion connoisseur. But I never thought a gown seemed very practical for riding a horse or walking in the hills. It appears the woman has abandoned her shoes, though." He pointed to a patch of dusty, scalped prairie less than a dozen feet outside the fence. "Somebody with small stockinged feet is walking with two booted men, who won't find it pleasant walking on this rough ground, either. Doesn't take a Comanche to track them, for now anyway. Look at the path in the grass."

The tallgrass looked like a giant snake had carved a path though it, weaving into the hills to the northeast. Kirsten said, "I think I know where they're headed. Herman and Gertie Gerhardt's. A sweet old couple. They came here from Illinois and homesteaded after the war. Their only child, Hans, died at Shiloh, and I guess they moved to Kansas for a fresh start. Hardworking folks who came to America with the first wave of German immigrants. Their quarter section would be about three miles from here."

"Horses?"

"Oh, yes. Herman's got a few big draft horses for some creek bottom he farms, and then he's got three or four nice quarter horse mares that produce foals he raises and sells to local ranchers. He fills out his grassland with some mixed-breed cows and heifers. He has rented one of my Red Angus bulls the past few years to service his cows and heifers."

The image of the gentle couple flashed through her mind. "Oh, my God. They're such honest, kind-hearted people. We've got to get to that place before something terrible happens. We don't need to track these no-goods. Follow me."

Kirsten led the way as they hurried toward the Gerhardt farm, forced to slow occasionally to negotiate tricky shale-cluttered trails. When they reached a rise in the ground overlooking the farmstead, they paused and surveyed the scene below. It was like viewing an artist's pastoral painting. The fresh, white paint on the house and barn sparkled in the sun, and the grounds were mowed and manicured. A garden devoid of weeds still showed some green from late corn, beans and other vegetables. The surrounding pasture was far from over-grazed, and Kirsten would bet weeds were alien to the crop ground as well. The Gerhardts' spirits were merged with their land, and they cared for it and nurtured it with love—and prospered from their hard work and dili-gence. Kirsten could usually ride past a farm and tell if it was German-owned.

"Pretty place," Quincy said. "Mighty quiet down there."

"Yes, but something's not right."

"What do you mean?"

"I've never been out this way when one or both these folks weren't outside working on some project. A place doesn't get this way by wishing for it to happen."

"No, ma'am. And I agree. It's too quiet for a working farm."

"I'm worried, Quincy, about what we're going to find here. I think we'd better stake the horses and walk in."

"Let's be doing it."

The two dismounted, retrieved their firearms, and started walking slowly down the slope. As they neared the farm buildings, Quincy raised his arm, signaling a halt, and whispered, "Hear that?"

"What?"

"Voices. The barn. I think we should split up. You take the back. I'll go in the front. Don't go in till you hear my voice. And you will hear it."

Quincy had a deep, booming voice. Not just a preacher's voice—a powerful voice that gave him a commanding presence. Next to Thad, whose manner was almost opposite, one of calm and quiet competence, she gave Quincy Belmont's opinions more credence than any other man of her acquaintance. She would usually listen to these two. Any other men carried the burdens of proving their worth before she would give any serious consideration to their viewpoints.

They separated, and while Quincy walked slowly and deliberately across the farmyard toward the barn's entrance, Kirsten swung around the side, scaling the wooden corrals and crossing horse and cow lots to reach the back. When she turned the corner of the building, she stopped abruptly as she came face to face with the man called Reuben, who had a rifle raised and aimed at her midsection.

"Well, if this ain't my lucky day," he grinned, displaying a mouthful of half-rotted teeth. "Stepped out here to take me a piss and got cut-off mid-stream when I heard a critter in the corral. Turned out to be a sassy little filly."

Kirsten froze. She carried her Winchester in her left hand, and her right was free to draw the Colt, but all Reuben needed to do was squeeze the trigger. She scolded herself for moving like a damned ox through the corrals. "Where are Mister and Missus Gerhardt?" she asked.

"Inside. You are going to come join the party as soon as you put your guns down. First, the rifle. Just set it down beside you."

She obeyed.

"Now you just take the butt of that pistol with your little old fingers and pull it out of the holster and drop it on the ground."

She considered making a move for the Colt, diving for the ground and getting off a shot. But her good sense told her she was not a dime novel gunfighter, so she did what she was told, praying that Quincy would get her out of this mess.

"Now, you just open that barn door and step inside and say howdy to your friends."

Kirsten moved to the door and opened it and walked inside. She had expected to step into darkness, but the wide, open door at the opposite end of the barn and several windows admitted enough sunshine to provide a dusky light that enabled her to see the occupants. She was relieved to find that Herman and Gertie were alive. Herman held the reins of a bay mare in a stall where Cyrus Crabbe struggled to saddle the nervous animal. The ruddy-faced farmer, wearing bib overalls and straw hat, appeared to be making only a token effort to calm the horse.

Gertie, a tiny lady with wisps of white hair creeping from beneath her sun bonnet, stood beside a taller angular-faced woman, who was dressed in black and held a small pistol, likely a derringer, aimed at Gertie's chest. Gertie's pale blue eyes flashed anger more than fear. Kirsten was glad to see the German immigrants were not cowering before this scum. She also took note of the pitchfork sticking up from a stack of hay behind the women.

"We've got a visitor," Reuben called, giving Kirsten a shove that caused her to stumble forward and nearly fall.

Cyrus Crabbe came out of the stall, pulling a Colt .45 from his belt, and walked toward Kirsten and Reuben.

The scowl on his face told her that he was not pleased by this new development.

"You were with the Lockes when they came to the gate. Reuben, check outside and see if anyone else is with her. And don't engage in conversation. Take them out."

"Yes, sir. My pleasure."

Reuben sauntered to the front opening, obviously unconcerned about the possible presence of other uninvited guests.

Crabbe turned back to Kirsten. "What are you doing here, woman?"

"I was riding by to alert area farmers and ranchers that some people from the commune were trying to escape the law and to be on the lookout. I was obviously too late for these folks."

"Did you come alone?"

"Of course. Why would I need help to spread an alarm?"

"Seems strange—a woman riding alone around these parts."

"Not as strange as a man killing an innocent old medicine woman."

"She made a bad choice—tried to shoot me."

She wondered if he was aware that he had just made a confession.

He answered her unasked question. "I don't mind saying it. You and your friends will be dead when we leave this farm."

Reuben was returning from his investigation. "Nobody else out there, Lord."

"What's this woman got for a horse? We can take it. Somehow, I don't think she would be riding a nag."

"I didn't see no horse."

"Well, she sure as hell didn't walk here. Where's your horse, woman?"

"I thought something didn't look right on the place. Too quiet. So I tied him back down the trail and thought I'd sneak in and see what was happening. But Reuben here was too smart for me."

Reuben grinned. "Now you and me might just get to be good friends." He moved close enough she could smell his rancid breath. "Can we take her with us, Lord? Just long enough for us to get acquainted, so to speak?"

Crabbe ran his eyes up and down the length of her body, like a horse trader appraising a good mare. He was apparently considering Reuben's suggestion. Then he backed away, shaking his head negatively. "We don't have time for that. And I don't trust this bitch. Any woman who wears a gun belt is likely to be treacherous as a rattlesnake. We couldn't close our eyes for a minute or she'd be trying something. Put her away. Now. Then take care of the other two, and we'll saddle up and beat it out of here."

Reuben shrugged, "Seems a waste, but if you say so." He nudged Kirsten's abdomen with his rifle and moved his finger to the trigger when the rear barn door burst open, and Quincy stepped in with his shotgun upraised. Reuben wheeled toward him, and Kirsten dropped to the floor and rolled away, just before the explosion roared through the building and Reuben's belly turned to bloody mush.

Kirsten scooted toward Reuben's fallen Winchester. She heard gunshots and saw Quincy duck behind the buckboard. Crabbe had made a dash for the saddled horse in the stall and had fired some wild shots at Quincy, whose view of Crabbe was now blocked. She snatched up the rifle, and in a sitting position waited for the commune leader to emerge from the stall. He did not disappoint and momentarily appeared, leading the bay and hurrying to the open barn door. She squeezed the trigger and fired a bullet into his right buttocks. Cranking another bullet into the chamber, she launched another missile into the left cheek to give him a matched pair. Crabbe released the mare's reins and dropped to the ground, rolling in the dirt and squealing like a pig.

Then she became aware of a woman screaming hysterically and turned her head in the direction of the screams, which had subsided to sobs now. She had feared Gertie Gerhardt had been shot by Agatha Crabbe during the melee, but the screamer was Agatha, who lay facedown while Gertie pulled the tines of the pitchfork from her back. Herman stood beside her and took the pitchfork from her with one hand and patted her shoulder consolingly with the other.

Then she said, "She was trying to shoot Mister Belmont and forgot about me. I didn't know what else to do. Gott in Himmel, I have never killed anyone before. I will surely go to hell now. Ja?"

Kirsten knelt beside Agatha and took her pocket knife and cut away the fabric from the wounds, finding three nasty punctures in her lower back. "No, Gertie, you didn't kill her. I don't think the tines sunk deeply enough to hit any vital organs." She wondered, though, what complications the wounds might bring. The pitchfork had no doubt cleared horse and cow manure from the barn floor in addition to tossing hay and spreading straw in the stalls. Thad had explained that since the Civil War, physicians had learned that deaths from many wounds were more likely to be caused from bacteria and organisms that triggered infections than the actual wounds themselves.

After examining Crabbe and confiscating the man's firearm, Quincy joined Kirsten at Agatha's side. "I think the so-called Lord will live, but you sure took away the man's dignity. How about this lady?"

Kirsten stood. "Short term she should make it. There's not a lot of bleeding, but punctures like this can turn serious. We need to get them both to a doctor."

"I think Thad has dealt with enough today. We should take them to a doctor in Manhattan. Doc Kleeb ought to be good enough for this pair. He's going to have to don his coroner's hat to look at what's left of this big man, I suppose."

"Yeah, even Kleeb can probably figure out the cause of death on that one."

Kirsten turned to Herman Gerhardt, who had seemed to watch the brief skirmish in stunned silence and was now consoling his wife. "Herman, can we borrow your buckboard and team to take these people to Manhattan? I'll see that the wagon and horses are cared for at the livery and arrange for their return in a few days."

"Of course. We owe you our lives. Take anything that will help."

Chapter 40

IT WAS NEARLY sundown when Kirsten and Quincy pulled the buckboard with its pitiful cargo up in front of the sheriff's office. Without a word, Kirsten and Quincy carried Agatha into the office and awakened the young deputy who had been snoozing at his desk. He was the same deputy who had assisted the sheriff at the commune, and he started to protest when Kirsten opened the door that led to the rows of jail cells.

Kirsten cut him short, "I lived here a spell. I'm familiar with the accommodations. Why don't you go tell your boss we're leaving prisoners and a corpse? You might want to fetch Doc Kleeb, too."

They placed Agatha on a cot in a cell across the hall from her son's. Timothy appeared to be sleeping and unaware of the newcomers. After moaning most of the journey, Agatha now slept, also. Whether it was the result of coma or exhaustion, Kirsten did not know and did not much care. Crabbe was fully awake, shrieking with pain when they tried to move him off the wagon, and he resisted with flailing arms until Quincy threatened to knock him senseless. After they dropped him on a cot in another cell, they unloaded Reuben's body. This was more difficult, not only because his weight was not far under three hundred pounds, but the corpse had stiffened with rigor mortis. They finally decided to drag him in by his feet.

Kirsten proposed hoisting the body upon the sheriff's desk, but Quincy would have no part of it, so they laid Reuben out just in front of the desk.

"Quincy," Kirsten said, "I can handle this from here if you want to head back home. Maybe you could drop off the team and wagon at the livery on your way. Tell the stable boy I'll take care of the bill. I'll hitch my horse out front and then wait for Mallery."

"Well, I'm sure Rachael and the girls have been doing chores, but it's quite a job, and I might be able to help finish up. Besides, I don't relish being a part of your conversation with the good sheriff."

"I have something else I'd like to talk about. Let's go on outside, and we can chat while I untie my horse from the wagon."

He looked at her quizzically. "Sure, we can do that."

A scowling Sheriff Sam Mallery arrived as Quincy was pulling out with the team and wagon. "Now what?" Mallery asked when he met Kirsten outside the office door.

"I brought in some criminals for you, Sheriff. Somebody's got to do it."

"You know, lady, you are becoming one big pain in the ass."

"Maybe your ass wouldn't hurt so much if you got off it once in a while."

The sheriff entered the office and she followed.

"What in the hell have you done to my office?"

"I didn't know where else to put him, Sam. Sorry the floor got messed up. There are two more in cells. They need a doctor as soon as possible."

"I sent Homer for Doc Kleeb. He told me about the two in back. He didn't say nothing about the corpse being here."

"We brought Reuben in after the deputy left. He's not responsible."

Doctor Kleeb came through the open doorway trailed by the deputy. "Go on back to the cells," Mallery said, "you can't help this one."

Kleeb looked aghast at the mutilated body stretched out on the floor and hurried away with the deputy.

"Do you want to hear about what happened?" Kirsten asked.

"I suppose I got no choice."

Kirsten gave the sheriff a shortened version of her and Quincy's confrontation with the Crabbes and Reuben. "I'm sure you will want to interview Herman and Gertie. They will confirm what I told you. They may have heard Cyrus Crabbe confess to Granny Gray Owl's murder as well. I suspect Reuben killed George Stewart. The others might shed some light on that, but there's no way to know if they're telling the truth. That's for you and the prosecuting attorney to figure out."

"I suppose you're going to talk to the newspapers about this?"

"I have no interest in talking to the newspapers. You can stretch the truth to suit you. But if Quincy and I are ever required to testify in court, we'll be telling the whole truth and nothing but the truth. Keep that in mind when you come up with your story."

"Are you insinuating I'm a liar?"

"My dad used to say about a man like you that he was as shy of the truth as a goat is of feathers."

"I don't understand."

"That doesn't surprise me."

Chapter 41

AFTER KIRSTEN LEFT the sheriff's office, she considered taking a hotel room for the night, but she felt a need to talk to Thad. It was about eight o'clock. She thought she should check in with Vedette and see if there was a report on Cam and whether Myles had returned home. If she spent an hour there, she could still be in Medicine Wheel by ten-thirty. She had another loose end. Where was Marty? Thad would know. She had a proposal for the girl, and she had to tell Marty about it.

Kirsten found chaos when she arrived at the Locke residence, but it was welcome chaos. Vedette beamed when she answered Kirsten's rapping at the door. "Kirsten," she said, "come in. We've all been worried about you. Marty is nearly crazed."

"Marty's here?"

"Come in and see for yourself."

Kirsten followed Vedette into the house and was surprised to find a parlor full of people. Myles and Marty sat at the dining table watching Gina draw on some old parchment. Ned sat on the settee, chatting with his mother, Serena. The redolent scent of fresh-baked cookies intermingled with brewing coffee wafted in from the kitchen. It was a relaxed domestic scene, and Kirsten took it as a sign that Cam had come through his surgery well. "How's Cam?" Kirsten asked Vedette.

"Myles reports he is doing well. Pilar and several ranch hands were to move him to the Circle L since Thad had no accommodations for human patients. Thad will ride over to the ranch to check on him, but Myles said Cam was already becoming his usual obstinate self, and he is confidant of his son's recovery."

"Did he say anything about Cinder?"

"Her status is less certain. Her surgery took much longer than Cam's, according to Myles. Thad's trying to save her leg. But she's alive, and he's watching her in case he must take the leg yet. Myles says Thad loves that dog like family."

"He does," Kirsten said, adding, "we both do."

Marty looked up and saw Kirsten. Squealing with excitement, she leaped up from her chair and raced across the room, almost knocking Kirsten over when she collapsed into her arms, sobbing with joy. "Oh, Kirsten. I was so afraid. Chief Red came by the clinic and said you and Mister Belmont had gone after Lord Cyrus and Agatha and Reuben. They're terrible people, and I didn't know what might have happened."

Kirsten held her close. There was something about this not-quite-woman that called on her instincts to protect her. More of the maternal stuff? "I'm fine," she said. "And the Crabbes are in jail. Reuben is dead."

Serena and Ned joined them as Kirsten released Marty. She turned to Serena. "And your father is okay, Serena. We brought the prisoners to the jail and he headed home not more than a half hour ago. Said he needed to help with chores. He saved my life, by the way. He's a warrior."

"Yes. We had our differences once, but that's long past. I love and respect my father. I'm proud to be his daughter."

"Let's take over the table," Vedette said. "While we're all together, there are things we should talk about."

"I agree," Kirsten said.

When they were all seated at the table, except for Gina, who was absorbed with her drawing and uninterested in the adult conversation and found her own niche on the floor, Vedette took charge. "Kirsten, you might be relieved to know that the local churches have formed an alliance to help the folks at the commune. The local Friends congregation and the African Second Baptist already have members out there with food and clothing. I will be going out to the commune tomorrow with some others from my church, the African Second Methodist. The white Methodist preacher is organizing his congregation to help, and the Presbyterians are committed. They have offered a large social building adjacent to their church to house the refugees. It will be easier to manage the crisis if they can get everybody moved to town."

"That's a huge relief. I was hoping somebody would take over."

"That brings us to the next matter," Vedette said. "Marty and Gina were with the commune, but neither has any relatives there."

Myles interrupted, "I have discussed it with Vedette. Gina and I have formed something of a bond. She is going to remain with us, and we will raise her. She has been told and, as you can see, she has already settled in. We have told Marty she is welcome to stay with us." He smiled at Marty. "But she wanted to speak with you before making a commitment."

Marty, who was sitting next to Kirsten, looked at her uncertainly and shrugged.

Kirsten said, "If she is willing, I would like to have Marty come live with me. I can't replace her mother, but I will be her devout friend. I will see she gets some meat on her bones, and I will be responsible for her education. And she will always have a place she can call home."

"Yes, thank you," Marty said, leaning her head against Kirsten's shoulder and clutching her arm. "I'll never be a problem. I promise."

Kirsten laughed. "Yes, you will. But I'll love you anyway. Vedette. Myles. Could Marty stay here for three or four days? We'll likely live at my ranch, but I have a lot of arrangements to make."

Vedette said, "We would love to have her, and, if she is going to high school in Manhattan when she's ready, she would be welcome to stay here just like Thad and Hannah did."

"Thank you. Myles, I would like to employ your firm to take care of any legal matters to establish my guardianship over Marty."

"Of course. I'll take care of it personally."

"Now, I need to be moving on. I hope to get back to Medicine Wheel to talk with Thad yet tonight. I have some important information for him."

Serena had been silent to this point, but now she spoke. "Kirsten, I had hoped to speak with Thad by now, but all of this trouble came up. I should do this personally, but time is running short." She related her plans to be travelling the country on behalf of the Bill of Rights Society for some months. "I will, of course, be in Manhattan for short periods during that time and will see Ned then, but I thought this might be a good time for him to really spend daily time with his father. I know Ned's excited about it. He could stay with my folks, and Myles and Vedette said he would be welcome here. Do you think this would work out for Thad?"

"Thad is one person I generally avoid speaking for. But I know Thad will be ecstatic. Do you want me to talk to him?"

"I would appreciate it. I won't leave for another week, and I should be in the office during that time, if he would stop in and work out the details with me."

"I'll tell him. I'm glad Thad's a natural stoic. The news I'm carrying tonight might panic a lesser man."

Chapter 42

THAD WAS IN the kennel room checking on Cinder when he heard the rattling of the door lock from the front office. Elizabeth and Kirsten were the only other persons who possessed keys to the clinic, and Elizabeth would be home at the Belmont farm at this hour. He figured Kirsten would see the lamplight coming from the kennel and come on back.

The thought that she was here buoyed his spirits. The last few days had been grueling, but her presence almost always gave him peace, which he thought strange given her forceful personality. Then it occurred to him that while she could be counted on to speak her mind, she never pushed him or tried to order him around. And, if there was one person he could count on to always cover his back, it was Kirsten Cavelle.

He was kneeling by the floor-level cage, scratching Cinder gently behind her ears when Kirsten walked into the room. Kirsten knelt beside him and placed a hand on his shoulder. "How is she?" Kirsten asked.

"She's being a good girl. Doesn't struggle to get to her feet much. Stretches out in her cage."

"You're emotionally involved with your patient."

"Yeah, I guess I am."

"What about her leg?"

"No sign of infection so far. I need to keep it clean and wrapped for a few weeks. I'm going to fashion a collar out of one of the stiff leather fire hats that should keep her from reaching the bandages to chew off. I really thought I'd have to amputate, but we've got a good chance of saving the leg. She'll be left with a limp, but better than being three-legged—although dogs that are short a leg get along amazingly well."

"Is it okay if I stay over tonight? I'm too tired to ride home."

"You know it is."

"I'd like to talk, too. Serious stuff."

"Sounds ominous."

"Not really. Or I hope you don't think so."

"Why don't you go on upstairs, and I'll get Cinder a fresh bowl of water and get her tucked in."

By the time Thad got upstairs, Kirsten had stripped off her clothes and lay naked under the covers.

"I thought we were going to talk," he teased.

"We are. Any reason we can't be comfortable?"

"You make it difficult for me to focus on conversation."

"You can focus when you hear what I've got to say."

"Now I'm really getting curious." He started to undress and was down to his shirt and underwear when he noticed her shoulder. He tugged the blanket off her shoulders to her waist. "Let me look at your back." She rolled over and lay face-down. "You've got some nasty burns on your left shoulder and upper back. Did that happen when we were in the barn?"

"Yeah."

"Why didn't you say something?"

"We've both been busy."

"Well, they haven't blistered. I've got some salve in the cupboard I used on my arm. It will ease the pain and help healing. We can't have damage to that beautiful back." He got up and retrieved a tin of a white salve and sat down again and began rubbing it very gently on the raw flesh.

"Very nice," she purred. "I hope you don't put me to sleep."

"That's okay."

"No. We've got to talk. What is this stuff anyway?"

"One of Granny's concoctions. I use it on sore cow udders."

"My udders are fine. Just on the small side."

"You have perfect udders. Now let me put this away. I'll give you another treatment in the morning."

He finished undressing and joined her under the thin blanket. "Are we still going to talk?"

"Absolutely." She turned over on her side and snuggled against him, tossing her arm over her chest.

"What are we going to talk about?"

"The winds of change."

"What does that mean?"

"Changes may be coming to our lives."

"For example?"

"I'm going to have a daughter."

"You're pregnant?"

Kirsten giggled. "No. But Marty is going to come live with me. I will be her guardian until she is of age."

He did not know what to make of her announcement. He supported the decision. Kirsten and Marty had instantly bonded. They could be very good for each other. It might make maintenance of his relationship with Kirsten a bit trickier. "I'm glad for you both," he said.

"I spoke with Serena. She has accepted a position that will require her to make living arrangements for Ned for three or four months, perhaps as many as six. She plans to ask you if he could live with you during that time."

The idea thrilled him. An opportunity to be a day to day father to the son who was absent from his life for so many years. "Of course. Why would she even doubt he would be welcome at my place? I'll have to work out some changes at the ranch house. I only have one bedroom, and he's been sleeping on a straw mattress on the parlor floor when he visits weekends and summer stretches. I have a lot of things to figure out. I could make changes to the old vet office that was a part of the house. He could take my bedroom, and I could move in there."

"He could stay at my place. Since I built on to the house, I have three bedrooms."

"That would be ridiculous. He's going to live with me."

"But you could live there, too, and we would share a bedroom."

"What kind of example would that be with young folks in the house? I wouldn't feel right about it."

"That could be resolved. Last spring you asked me to marry you. I said I'd have to think about that. I've thought about it. Is the offer still good?"

"Of course it is. But I had about given up on you."

Ron Schwab

She scooted up on the bed, raising her face above his.

"I was a fool to hesitate. I love you, Thad Locke. We've been business partners and friends, and, yes, lovers for several years. Now I'm ready to be your partner in life. Yes, I want to marry you. Soon." She kissed him almost chastely on the lips and moved back and cradled her head in his arm.

"Soon? How soon?"

"Saturday noon."

"But this is Wednesday night. We'd only have two days to make arrangements."

"We would have to go to the courthouse tomorrow and take care of the license paperwork. Quincy has said he will preside at the fire hall Saturday noon. We can invite the volunteers by ringing the bell a half hour before reciting the vows. I'll pass the word through the grapevine to the wives. I don't have any family nearby, and I'll give myself away. I'm sure you would want to invite your father and Vedette—probably Cam, if he is able, and certainly Pilar and the kids."

"We would need to prepare food."

"I have agreed to make a generous donation to Quincy's Flint Hills Church if his church folks prepare and serve the food. We have ample tables and chairs at the hall."

"Is there anything you haven't thought of?"

"I doubt it," she said drowsily, her voice suddenly trailing off.

He started to ask her another question but saw that her eyes had closed, and she was snoring very softly, something like a cat purring. He loved this woman and had no doubt they would be true partners in life. But he had no illusions. Every morning when he woke up in bed with Crazy Kirsten would be the start of a new adventure.

Chapter 43

MYLES LOCKE SPOKE briefly with Thad when his son stopped by the Locke & Locke offices to visit with Serena about Ned's living arrangements. He was only mildly surprised when Thad informed him of his plans to wed Kirsten in two days. He assured his son that he, Vedette, and Gina would attend the event. He did not mention that Vedette had also come around since his near death, and they would likely follow Thad and Kirsten to the altar before Christmas. A child had also contributed to that decision. Vedette, though, still was not without reservations regarding the social consequences of their interracial marriage.

Myles also had informed Thad of Granny Gray Owl's burial at her beloved farm the next day, and Thad assured him he, and, likely, Kirsten would be present. Myles was scheduled to meet with Granny's nephew in a half hour, and he hoped the nephew would be receptive to a treasure hunt following the services.

While he waited for his appointment with Thomas Penn, he thumbed through the latest issue of the Manhattan Nationalist. The front page was virtually covered with stories about Peace Commune and the murders and attempted atrocities by its leaders. Sheriff Sam Mallery was the primary source of information for all the stories. Myles's imprisonment was briefly mentioned. He had been contacted but declined comment. Mallery asserted that the criminals had been apprehended and one killed, the implication being that this had all been accomplished by the local sheriff's department. Some of the truth would leak out if trials ensued, but Myles knew that Quincy, Thad, and Kirsten all preferred anonymity and would not initiate any action to correct the news stories. Sheriff Mallery was, of course, betting on this.

Myles just wanted to get back to the practice of law and carving out more time to spend with Vedette and Gina. If he had learned anything from his flirtation with death, it was that his work as a preeminent attorney meant little when weighed against the quality of his ties to family and others he cared about. He supposed he was too old to greatly change the habits of a lifetime, but he was determined to do his best.

Reva broke into his reverie when she entered the office and informed him that Mister Thomas Penn had arrived. "Send him in," Myles said. "It's about time I met Granny's nephew."

Shortly, a man with bronze-tinted skin and short-cropped black hair entered the room. He was a trim man of average height, professionally attired in a dark, pin-striped suit. Myles guessed he would be in his mid-thirties. His Kaw ancestry was evident to one who knew his heritage, but to a stranger he might have been descended from Italian or Spanish bloodlines. Women would likely take notice of him, Myles suspected.

Myles stepped around his desk and extended his hand, which was accepted with a firm grip. "Mister Penn, I'm Myles Locke—please call me Myles."

"I'm Tom. A pleasure to meet you. Aunt Amelia spoke very highly of you. She trusted you, and that's saying a lot, because she did not have a trusting nature."

"Please accept my condolences on your tragic loss, Tom. Be seated, and I'll bring you up to date on what I've done to this point and the arrangements your aunt made."

"I appreciate that you have taken care of all the funeral details. I stopped at the undertaker's, and it seems there is little for me to do."

"My secretary, Reva, actually took charge of arrangements. I've been out of the office most of the time since Amelia's death . . . but that's another story."

"Since I arrived in town yesterday, I've heard snippets about your misfortune. I'm just glad you are here to help me."

"You are aware, I gather, that your aunt did not want a public funeral and that she is to be buried on the farm tomorrow. I have invited my son, Thad, and his soon-to-be bride to be present. He was a special friend of your aunt's and is to take over my responsibilities regarding the estate when I am no longer able. Amelia did not have a church affiliation I know of, but I do have a preacher I could call on if you want some graveside words."

"That won't be necessary. I telegraphed a friend at the Kaw reservation in Oklahoma. There should be two holy men arriving on the afternoon train."

"Oh, very well. But Amelia was not blood Kaw, was she?"

Penn smiled. "No, her and my grandfather's side of the family emigrated to America by way of England as Quakers of French Huguenot descent. She and my grandfather, who was her brother, came west to Kansas to establish a mission among the Kaw. My grandfather married a Kaw woman, and, ironically, the missionaries eventually converted to the Kaw religion. Amelia, who was my great-aunt, adopted the Kaw culture, took a Kaw name and developed an interest in medicinal plants and remedies used by the various Indian tribes. As a result, she became something of a medicine woman among the Kaw."

"But she did not go to the reservation with the Kaw?"

"She and my grandfather and grandmother went to the first reservation established south of here near Council Grove, but they and my grandparents' son—my father—did not go with the tribe when the reservation was moved to Oklahoma. Several families of mixed blood remained in Kansas, including my mother's. She was also half-blood. My grandparents died during a cholera epidemic, but my father and his new half-blood wife joined Amelia on the farm near what is now Medicine Wheel, where I was raised until I was twelve. At that time, my parents took me and my little sister east to St. Louis. My father was a skilled carpenter and craftsman and thought he could find more opportunities there. I suppose he did, but my sister died from diphtheria a year later, and my mother died five years after that."

"How sad. But I understand you are an architect, so you obviously found educational advantages and a career there."

"Yes, and my father gained respect and modest prosperity as a craftsman. He never remarried and died a bit over five years ago. I've always wondered what would have happened if we had just stayed here. My heart never really left the Flint Hills anyway."

"A person's life is always filled with 'what ifs.' It's a long chain of choices, any one of which may change the story of one's time on this earth. And there are no rewrites."

Penn was silent a moment and then nodded. "Yes, that's true."

Myles said, "I must tell you about the circumstances of your aunt's death. It's not a pleasant story."

"The undertaker was very mysterious about it all."

"I feared you might have read newspaper accounts before we spoke. I am sorry to tell you she was murdered."

"Murdered? Who would want to kill Aunt Amelia?"

Myles gave him a nutshell version of the circumstances known about Granny's death and the events following.

Penn shook his head in disbelief. "It had to be terrible for Aunt Amelia. It's hard to think of her dying that way."

"I understand." Myles turned the conversation to the purpose of their meeting. "I would like to review your aunt's will with you. There are some unusual provisions." He took a letter opener and broke the wax seal on the will envelope, removed the document, and passed it to Penn and gave him a few minutes to read it. His face was impassive, so Myles could not gauge the young architect's reaction.

Penn handed the will back. "Aunt Amelia discussed her plans with me when I visited several years ago. She knew that I had no financial concerns and, also, that I hoped to return to the Flint Hills someday. That's likely why she left me the farm. I wish I had returned sooner to spend more time with her, but as you said, there are no rewrites."

"Did you know that she was extremely wealthy? She held stock in many thriving companies. Her trust fund will be very well-endowed."

"I had no idea. I wondered how she was going to fund a trust. And I must confess I am more than just a little curious about the goat pen can."

"If you do not find it disrespectful to your aunt, we will go on a treasure hunt after the burial tomorrow."

"Aunt Amelia would love it. She had a rather strange sense of humor sometimes, and I think she's up there some place laughing about this. And I'll bet we're not going to find a pot of gold."

Chapter 44

GRANNY GRAY OWL'S graveside services were at once simple and unconventional, Thad thought. The burial spot had been on top of a tallgrass-covered knoll and was within sight of the former residence. Tom Penn had accompanied the undertaker, Harley Richardson, and two gravediggers with the pine coffin to the farm early morning and selected the burial site overlooking the forty-acre tract. Two elderly Kaw Indians had followed on horses rented from the local livery.

Myles, accompanied by Ned, had arrived by carriage in Medicine Wheel earlier and was joined by Thad and Kirsten on the journey to the farm. By the time they arrived late morning, the rhythmic sound of a tom-tom's beat echoed through the hills. They tied their horses to some tree branches near the lodge ruins and walked to the burial site and met up with Tom Penn and the under-taker and his gravediggers.

The loin-clothed, bare-chested Kaw drummer sat on the earth a short distance from the open grave, a drum wedged between naked thighs. Thad wondered if the wizened man might be considered a medicine man, given the buffalo-horned headdress he wore. There was no question that the other Indian was a chief or man of rank. Attired in fringed buckskins and an eagle feather headdress with a trailer that stretched to his ankles, he stood near the drummer with arms upraised and eyes gazing skyward. He chanted and sang for some minutes before bending over and clutching a handful of freshly-dug dirt and sprinkling it on the coffin. Abruptly, the drumming halted.

Penn nodded to the undertaker, who asked Thad to take the end of one of two ropes, and they lowered the coffin into the ground. As the Lockes and Kirsten walked away from the gravesite, Thad noticed Penn remained behind and was apparently settling some financial busi-ness with the Kaw. The undertaker did not signal the diggers to fill the grave until Penn joined Thad's group and the Kaw mounted their horses and rode away.

When Penn walked up, Myles introduced his guests to the architect. As he shook Ned's hand, Penn said, "So you're the young man Serena spoke about."

Ned replied, "You know my mom?"

"I do." He turned to Myles. "I didn't get to tell you, Myles. I encountered Serena in your reception area when I was leaving your office, and Reva introduced us. We started talking and I invited her to join me for dinner. She said Ned here was staying at your house for a few days, so she accepted. A very, very impressive woman."

Thad thought the guy was overdoing it a bit, but he supposed Penn had not expected to find a lady of Serena's polish and sophistication in the Flint Hills cow country.

Myles said, "She's a lawyer of great skill, and we're very fortunate to have her in the office."

Then, speaking to Thad and Kirsten, Penn said, "And I understand congratulations are due the two of you. Serena said you are to be married tomorrow."

"Yes," Kirsten replied. "Why don't you join the festivities—such as they are. If you plan to move here, it would be an opportunity to meet some of your neighbors. It will be a very informal affair, but the food will be the best you'll find in these parts. Perhaps you could come with Serena."

With Thad's approval Kirsten had invited Serena to their nuptials. The women were fast friends, and he decided that was a good thing since Kirsten would soon be stepmother of Serena's son. Serena had been his first love, but too many years had passed since the summer interlude that produced their child. And he could forgive but not forget the lost years during which Serena had withheld the information he had fathered a child. Their time had faded to fond remembrance, and any lingering embers of love had finally been smothered by harsh realities resulting from the differing paths their lives had taken.

"That might be nice. I would welcome the opportunity to meet some folks, and it would be a chance for me to speak with Serena again. I will need to wind down my business in St. Louis over the next six months, and it appears Serena will be leaving Manhattan for an extended time. I am definitely moving out on this place, and I'm gambling there will be work for an architect in this area."

"No competition I am aware of," Thad said. "And as the college expands, it seems there would be possibilities there even without the anticipated growth of Manhattan."

"I'll make a market."

Kirsten laughed. "That's my motto."

Myles interrupted. "Folks, I promised Gina I would come directly home when my business here was finished. Perhaps we should make a search of the goat pen. It looks like Harley and the diggers are about finished at the gravesite. I asked him to leave the shovels behind and said I would bring them with me when I return to Manhattan."

Chapter 45

A T LEAST THE goat and mule dung had mostly dried-out in the pen and adjacent shed. Thad guessed the pen was about twenty feet wide and forty feet long. Both his father and Tom Penn wore business suits and were hardly attired for the dirty work. Thad, Kirsten, and Ned had worn their best boots and clean denim blue jeans and cotton shirts. Thad handed Ned one of the shovels, and he kept the other.

"Dad," Thad asked, "did Granny leave any other clues about where this can might be found in the goat pen? We'll be at this for days if we have to dig up the entire pen."

"Nothing. Just a can in the goat pen."

Penn said, "There is a hidden riddle or something here. Aunt Amelia was having fun. It's a game. I think one of us knows something about her or this little farm that would lead us to it. That person just doesn't know she or he knows it. Am I making sense?"

"I understand what you are saying," Thad said. "But how do we identify the person and the knowledge?"

Kirsten said, "You are the person, Thad. Can't you see that? She gave whatever we are looking for to you. She was playing the game with you."

"That does make some sense, I guess."

Thad started pacing the goat pen, testing the ground randomly with his shovel, and Ned soon followed his father's example.

Kirsten leaned up against the fence. "Thad, have you been in this pen before?"

He paused and considered her question. "Yes, twice. Goats tend to get along without much veterinary assistance, but, knowing that Granny could not physically load up an animal and bring it to the clinic, I had assured her when I made one of my medicine visits that I would make a house call if she would get word to me about any help she needed. I guess it was about three years ago, she came in with her wagon and said she had a nanny having trouble birthing a kid. I remember it because I had never helped with goat kidding before."

"Did you pull a live kid?"

"As a matter of fact, I did. That's my greatest satisfaction—delivering a live calf or foal or, in this case, a kid. The nanny would have died without help. A front leg of the kid was bent back, blocking exit, but I straightened out the leg, and the kid slipped out without much help after that. A little doe baby, as I recall. It was one of the few times I'd seen Granny smile. But our next adventure she actually laughed."

"Tell us about the next adventure," Kirsten prodded.

"She set up an appointment for me to come out and wether a big buck."

"Wether?"

"Castrate. Like steering a bull. The bull becomes a steer, and a goat becomes a wether."

"Sounds rather demeaning," Penn said.

"I suppose they feel demeaned. I know this one did. Granny usually sold off the bucks with cull females and held onto the best does and nannies, but this guy was a pet—'Chief,' she called him. She couldn't let him go, but all the young does were his progeny, and she didn't want him breeding and impregnating his daughters. She had already arranged for purchase of a new breeding buck, but we had to get Chief castrated and accepting his fate before breeding season and introducing his successor into the herd. As luck would have it, we had a gully-washing rain the day before I came out, so the lot here was like thick soup. Then I had to rope Chief and get him snugged up to the fence before I worked on him."

"Roping a goat. Now that's something I've never done," Kirsten said.

"It wasn't easy. That devil was big, strong, and fast. I tossed several misses before I caught him, and when I finally did, instead of running he wheeled and charged. He drove his head and horns into my chest and sent me sprawling in the mud. I must have looked like a damned rodeo clown. I guess Granny thought so because she laughed till tears streamed from her eyes. I went down at least two more times before I had him hitched tight to a post. Then I got behind him and tried to do the surgery, and he kicked and bucked, so I couldn't get my knife to his scrotum. I finally got another rope and looped it under his belly and over his hips and cinched him to the fence. After that, I relished taking the knife to his balls and had the job done in less than a minute. Granny wanted me to save one of the testicles for her to roast and the other . . . my God, why didn't I think of that before?"

"What are you talking about?" Kirsten asked.

"The other testicle. She asked me to bury it in the pen."

"And you did it? Why on earth would you bury a goat's nut in the goat pen?"

"It had to do with fertility. I guess he was an exceptional buck—sired superior kids. She said his passionate spirit would remain here and assure successful mating in perpetuity."

Kirsten groaned in disbelief. "Well, I'm sure that was a lot of consolation to poor old Chief. But you may be on to something. So where did you bury the nut? Of course, all that's left by now is its spirit."

Thad tried to reconstruct the scene in his mind. "It wasn't far from the fence." He pointed to the southwest corner. "I think it was near that corner post."

He walked toward the corner of the lot, glad that the earth had baked to dry dust this day. He and Ned began digging. After they peeled off the layers of decaying manure, the ground gave way easily to the shovel blades. He would have expected to strike stones and difficult digging. Ned's shovel blade clanged as it struck metal.

"I've hit something, Dad," Ned said.

Thad took his shovel and began to scrape away the dirt from the object. It appeared to be a large tin canister. The top of the container was no more than six inches below the surface. A goat's foot probably wouldn't have broken through the surface, but the old mule could have been a hazard. The others gathered around with curious eyes as he knelt and worked the canister out of its burial place.

"It's not gold," Thad said as he pulled it from the hole. "It weighs next to nothing." He tapped on the rust-spotted container, which he guessed was about fourteen inches tall and eight inches in diameter. His reply was a hollow, tinny echo. "You said your aunt had a strange sense of humor, Tom. Perhaps its empty."

The lid appeared rusted to the canister top, but after pounding on it sharply with his fist, he finally twisted it free and removed it. A loose bundle of parchment papers was rolled up inside, nearly filling the canister. "Paper," Thad announced.

Ever the lawyer, Myles asked, "Stocks? Bonds?"

Thad plucked out a sheet, unrolled it and examined the page. He smiled. "It is a treasure. Recipes— prescriptions, if you will—for her medicines and herbal remedies. It looks like enough for a book's worth. I had feared they were lost forever."

Chapter 46

THAD LOOKED OUT of his loft apartment in the vet clinic and was surprised to see all the activity at the fire hall. Quincy Belmont had taken it upon himself to build cooking fires in the middle of the street and seemed to be barbecuing beef and pork. Countless Dutch ovens lay near the fires, their lids covered with hot coals. Tables covered with pies and other dishes were lined up just inside the hall's entrance. It appeared they were preparing to feed a battalion of soldiers. He was anticipating a small wedding, but somewhere the celebration had gotten out of control. He shook it off and decided it was out of his hands.

It was nearly ten o'clock. He had slept late this morning after awakening and hearing Elizabeth downstairs tending to the few patients hospitalized in the clinic over the weekend. She had asked yesterday if she might try to bring Cinder to the wedding for a spell, suggesting the Dalmatian should be moving on the crippled leg a bit now. He had consented.

After leaving Granny's place with his buried treasure mid-afternoon yesterday, Thad had learned his day was far from over. He had returned to his Medicine Wheel clinic to see if there were patients requiring his attention. Fortunately, Elizabeth had already sutured the wounds of a dog that foolishly tried to take on a bobcat. She had reported a cow with a calving problem, however. Conveniently, the patient was not far from his own ranch house, where he needed to retrieve clothes for his wedding. The rancher had been relieved when Thad showed up and even more so when the vet pulled a live calf.

Kirsten had suggested Thad stop by the C Bar C after he picked up his clothes. He had assumed he would spend the night there. No, that was not what his betrothed had in mind. In fact, Kirsten had brought Marty out from Manhattan and was moving the girl into her new bedroom. There were a half dozen boxes filled with new women's garments scattered about the living area. "Vedette, Marty, and Gina went shopping," Kirsten had explained.

"Are you wearing a dress?" Not a good question. She had reprimanded him with her patented glare.

She had shown him Marty's bedroom and then Ned's. They had been added to the house within the past year. "Marty's is a bit larger. I hope that's okay."

"I don't think Ned requires much space, and he will likely be here only part-time. I doubt if a twelve-year-old boy needs as much room as a sixteen-year-old girl anyway."

"And then there is our room," she said, leading him to the opposite end of the house.

"Notice anything?" she asked as they peered in.

"No."

"I had a lock installed."

"Oh."

"For more privacy."

"I understand."

"Of course, the kids will be at the other end of the house, and they are old enough that shouldn't be a problem."

"I would hope not. You may have to quiet down some when—"

She gave him a nudge in his ribs. "I'm not that noisy."

"Scares the hell out of the horses in the stable."

She had ignored his comment but had the last word. "We'll be spending our wedding night with two kids in the house."

"Yes, that's okay. It's not like it is the first time we've shared a bed."

"And, of course, we can't share it tonight—our not being married and Marty staying here. That wouldn't be proper. Besides, don't you think it would seem a bit strange to sleep together and then get up in the morning and go to our wedding."

"I hadn't thought about that. I guess I'd better be going."

Then she had grabbed him about the neck and pulled his head to hers and kissed him passionately, her body melting into his. "After tonight, Doc, you won't be able to keep me out of your bed . . . ever."

Then Marty's voice had broken into the moment. "Is there going to be a lot of this mush going on here?"

Kirsten had turned to her. "Oh, yes, Marty. But mostly behind closed doors."

Thad smiled as he thought of last night's visit to his new home. Every day of life with Kirsten would be a new adventure. He usually preferred routine, but he was ready for this journey. It was time.

By the time Thad bathed, shaved, and dressed, the fire bell was ringing, so he went downstairs and stepped through the clinic door and onto the boardwalk. He was nearly overwhelmed when he saw the crowd milling on the street. He could not even attach names to some of the faces. The wedding had turned into a county fair.

He was delighted, though, when he saw his Aunt Nancy and Uncle Eldridge Clay strolling his way. They had virtually raised him and his twin sister after his mother's death, and he felt a bit guilty he had not visited lately. He walked out to meet them, hugging his aunt and kissing her cheek and then shaking his uncle's hand. "I'm so glad you're here. No time for engraved invitations. Dad said he would get word to you."

"He did," his aunt said, "and nothing could have kept us away. We're so happy for you and Kirsten. I knew you'd get around to this sooner or later." She hesitated. "I assume you've got a wedding band for Kirsten?"

"Oh my God. Everything happened so fast, I hadn't even thought about it." A rare wave of panic struck him.

Aunt Nancy reached her hand into her bag and plucked something from it. She extended her hand, displaying a gold band in her palm. "This was your mother's. It may be a bit tight for Kirsten's finger, but a jeweler can fix that."

He accepted the ring and placed it in his coat pocket. "Thank you, Aunt Nancy. You've not only saved my hide, but I think Kirsten will be honored to wear my mother's band."

He heard a ruckus down the street and turned that way. A large two-seated carriage behind a team of white horses. Kirsten and Marty, with the former handling the reins. The crowd parted as they pulled up in front of the fire hall. Thad excused himself and walked out to greet and assist the ladies from the carriage. Marty, dressed in an elegant yellow gown and bonnet, first. Even Kirsten, probably for the first time in her life, waited for his assistance, and stepped gracefully from the carriage. They faced each other for a moment. She was stunning in the high-necked, pale-blue gown and tiara covered with assorted blue flowers and veil.

"You clean up good," Thad teased. "Seriously, you are the most beautiful woman in the world."

"Marrying the most handsome and dashing man." She leaned forward and whispered, "Ladies would have talked if I wore white."

He smiled and offered his arm, and they made their way to the front of the fire hall, where a black-suited Reverend Quincy Belmont waited. His daughter, Elizabeth, stood off to one side with Cinder and Socks.

Ned Locke stepped from the crowd to stand by his father, and Marty joined Kirsten. Gina, dressed in a gown that matched Marty's, emerged from the onlookers and presented a bouquet to the bride. Thad caught a glimpse of Serena, who stood beside Tom Penn. Their eyes met, and Serena smiled and winked. Then, Reverend Belmont got to the business at hand.

Made in the USA
Las Vegas, NV
13 September 2023

77527863R00187